PENGUIN CLASSICS
Maigret Hesitates

T0200779

'I love reading Simenon. He makes me think of Chekhov'
– William Faulkner

'A truly wonderful writer . . . marvellously readable – lucid,
simple, absolutely in tune with the world he creates'
– Muriel Spark

'Few writers have ever conveyed with such a sure touch, the
bleakness of human life' – A. N. Wilson

'One of the greatest writers of the twentieth century . . .
Simenon was unequalled at making us look inside, though
the ability was masked by his brilliance at absorbing us
obsessively in his stories' – *Guardian*

'A novelist who entered his fictional world as if he were part
of it' – Peter Ackroyd

'The greatest of all, the most genuine novelist we have had
in literature' – André Gide

'Superb . . . The most addictive of writers . . . A unique teller
of tales' – *Observer*

'The mysteries of the human personality are revealed in all
their disconcerting complexity' – Anita Brookner

'A writer who, more than any other crime novelist, combined
a high literary reputation with popular appeal'
– P. D. James

'A supreme writer . . . Unforgettable vividness'
– *Independent*

'Compelling, remorseless, brilliant' – John Gray

'Extraordinary masterpieces of the twentieth century'
– John Banville

ABOUT THE AUTHOR

Georges Simenon was born on 12 February 1903 in Liège, Belgium, and died in 1989 in Lausanne, Switzerland, where he had lived for the latter part of his life. Between 1931 and 1972 he published seventy-five novels and twenty-eight short stories featuring Inspector Maigret.

Simenon always resisted identifying himself with his famous literary character, but acknowledged that they shared an important characteristic:

> My motto, to the extent that I have one, has been noted often enough, and I've always conformed to it. It's the one I've given to old Maigret, who resembles me in certain points . . . 'Understand and judge not.'

Penguin is publishing the entire series of Maigret novels.

GEORGES SIMENON

Maigret Hesitates

Translated by HOWARD CURTIS

PENGUIN BOOKS

PENGUIN CLASSICS

UK | USA | Canada | Ireland | Australia
India | New Zealand | South Africa

Penguin Books is part of the Penguin Random House group of companies
whose addresses can be found at global.penguinrandomhouse.com.

Penguin
Random House
UK

First published in French as *Maigret hésite*
by Presses de la Cité 1968
This translation first published 2019
002

Copyright © Georges Simenon Limited, 1968
Translation copyright © Howard Curtis, 2019
GEORGES SIMENON ® Simenon.tm
MAIGRET ® Georges Simenon Limited
All rights reserved

The moral rights of the author and translator have been asserted

Set in 12.5/15 pt Dante MT Std
Typeset by Jouve (UK), Milton Keynes
Printed and bound in Great Britain by Clays Ltd, Elcograf S.p.A.

ISBN: 978-0-241-30419-8

www.greenpenguin.co.uk

MIX
Paper from
responsible sources
FSC® C018179

Penguin Random House is committed to a
sustainable future for our business, our readers
and our planet. This book is made from Forest
Stewardship Council® certified paper.

Maigret Hesitates

1.

'Hello, Janvier.'

'Morning, chief.'

'Good morning, Lucas. Good morning, Lapointe.'

When he got to Lapointe, Maigret couldn't help smiling, and not only because the young inspector was sporting a tight-fitting new suit, pale-grey with thin red flecks. Everyone was smiling that morning, in the streets, on the buses, in the shops.

The previous day, a Sunday, had been grey and windy, with squalls of cold rain that recalled winter, and now suddenly, even though it was only 4 March, they had woken to spring.

True, the sun was still a little acidic, the blue of the sky fragile, but there was a gaiety in the air and in the eyes of people in the streets, a kind of complicity, a joy in living and in rediscovering the delicious smell of Paris in the morning.

Maigret had come just in a jacket and had walked most of the way. Immediately on getting to his office, he had gone to the window and half opened it. The Seine, too, was a different colour, the red lines on the funnels of the tugboats more vibrant, the barges done up like new.

He had opened the door to the inspectors' room.

'Coming, boys?'

It was what they called the 'little briefing', to distinguish it from the real briefing, for which the heads of departments gathered in the commissioner's office at nine o'clock every morning. This one was just for Maigret's closest colleagues.

'Did you have a good day yesterday?' he asked Janvier.

'We took the children to see my mother-in-law in Vaucresson.'

Lapointe, embarrassed by his new suit – so early for the time of year – stood apart from the others.

Maigret sat down at his desk, filled a pipe and started going through the mail.

'This one's for you, Lucas. It's about the Lebourg case.'

He held out other documents to Lapointe.

'To be taken to the prosecutor's office.'

It was still too early to speak of foliage, but there was nevertheless a hint of pale green in the trees along the river.

There was no big case in progress, none of those cases that fill the corridors of the Police Judiciaire with reporters and photographers and are the cause of urgent telephone calls from the higher echelons. Nothing but routine. Cases to be followed up . . .

'A madman or a madwoman,' he announced, picking up an envelope on which his name and the address of Quai des Orfèvres were written in block capitals.

The envelope was white and of good quality. The stamp had been postmarked at the post office in Rue de Miromesnil. What struck Maigret first, when he took the sheet of paper out, was the paper itself, a beautiful thick vellum that wasn't the usual size. The top of it must have been cut off to remove an engraved letterhead, a task that had been carefully carried out with the help of a ruler and a well-sharpened blade.

The text, like the address, was in very regular block capitals.

'Maybe not a madman,' he grunted.

Detective Chief Inspector,
I do not know you personally but what I have read about your investigations and your attitude towards criminals inspires trust. This letter may surprise you, but please do not throw it in the wastepaper basket too quickly. It is neither a joke nor the work of a maniac.

You know better than I do that reality is sometimes far-fetched. A murder will be committed soon, probably in a few days. Perhaps by someone I know, perhaps by myself.

I am not writing to you to prevent the tragedy occurring. In a way, it is inevitable. But when it does take place, I would like you to know.

If you take me seriously, please place the following small ad in *Le Figaro* or *Le Monde*: 'K. R. Expect a second letter.'

I do not know if I will write it. I am very confused. Some decisions are hard to make.

I may see you one day, in your office, but by then we will be on different sides of the barrier.

Your devoted servant.

He had stopped smiling. With a frown, he let his gaze wander over the sheet of paper, then looked at his colleagues.

'No, I don't think this is a madman,' he repeated. 'Listen.'

He read out the letter slowly, emphasizing certain words. He had received letters of this kind before, but most of the time the language was less carefully chosen and usually certain phrases were underlined. Often, they were written in red or green ink, and many contained spelling mistakes.

Here, the hand had not shaken. The strokes were firm and unadorned, without any crossings-out.

He held the paper up to the light and read the watermark: *Morvan Vellum*.

Every year he received hundreds of anonymous letters. With few exceptions, they were written on cheap paper, the kind found in neighbourhood grocery stores, and occasionally the words had been cut out of newspapers.

'No specific threat,' he said in a low voice. 'An underlying sense of anxiety . . . *Le Figaro* and *Le Monde*, two newspapers read above all by the thinking middle classes . . .'

He again looked at the three of them.

'Will you take care of it, Lapointe? The first thing to do is get in touch with the paper manufacturer, who's presumably in the Morvan.'

'Got it, chief.'

This was the start of a case that was to give Maigret more trouble than many crimes that made the front pages of the newspapers.

'And place that ad.'

'In *Le Figaro*?'

'In both papers.'

A bell announced the briefing, the real one, and Maigret

walked to the commissioner's office with a file in his hand. Here, too, the open window let in the noises of the city. One of the chief inspectors was sporting a sprig of mimosa in his buttonhole and felt the need to explain:

'They're selling them in the street for charity.'

Maigret didn't mention the letter. His pipe tasted good. Casually observing the faces of his colleagues as they took turns at presenting their little cases, he mentally calculated the number of times he had participated in this ritual. Thousands.

But there had been many more times when he had envied the detective chief inspector who had been his superior in the old days – envied him because every morning he was admitted to the holy of holies. Mustn't it be wonderful to be head of the crime squad? He hadn't dared dream of it at the time, any more than Lapointe or Janvier, or even good old Lucas, dreamed of it today.

It had happened all the same, and in all the years it had lasted he had stopped thinking about it, except on a morning like this, when the air had a delicious taste and the din of the buses raised a smile rather than a curse.

Returning to his office an hour later, he was surprised to find Lapointe standing by the window. His fashionable suit made him look thinner, taller and much younger. Twenty years earlier, an inspector would not have been allowed to dress like this.

'It was almost too easy, chief.'

'You tracked down the paper manufacturer?'

'Géron and Son, who've owned the Morvan Mills in

7

Autun for three or four generations. It's not a factory, more of a cottage industry. The paper's made to measure, either for de luxe publications, especially poetry, apparently, or for writing paper. The Gérons only have about ten workers. From what they told me, there are still a number of paper mills like that in the region.'

'Do you have the name of their representative in Paris?'

'They don't have a representative. They work directly with publishers of art books and with two stationers, one in Rue du Faubourg Saint-Honoré, the other on Avenue de l'Opéra.'

'Right at the end of Faubourg Saint-Honoré, on the left?'

'I think so, judging by the number. Roman's Stationers.'

Maigret knew the shop from having often looked in the window, which was full of invitations and business cards, with names you didn't often hear these days:

The Count and Countess of Vaudry have the honour to . . .

The Baroness of Grand-Lussac is happy to announce . . .

Princes, dukes, genuine or not – you wondered if they still existed. They invited each other to dinners, hunting parties and bridge games, announced the marriage of their daughter or the birth of a baby, all this on luxury paper.

In the second window, there were emblazoned desk blotters and morocco-bound folders for daily menus.

'You'd better go and see them.'

'Roman's?'

'I have the feeling that's the right kind of neighbour-hood.'

The shop on Avenue de l'Opéra was distinguished, too, but also sold pens and standard stationery items.

'I'll go there now, chief.'

The lucky devil! Maigret watched him leave, like when, at school, a teacher had sent one of his classmates on an errand. He himself had only everyday chores to deal with, the usual paperwork, a report of no interest whatever for an examining magistrate who would file it away without reading it because the case had been hushed up.

The smoke from his pipe was starting to turn the air blue, and a very light breeze wafted in from the Seine, stirring the papers on the desk. By eleven o'clock, Lapointe was already back, exuberant and full of life.

'It's still too easy.'

'What do you mean?'

'It's as if that paper was chosen deliberately. By the way, Roman's Stationers is no longer run by Monsieur Roman, who died ten years ago, but by a Madame Laubier, a widow in her fifties who wouldn't let me go. She hasn't ordered paper of that quality for five years, because there are no buyers. Not only is it massively expensive, it's also hard to use in a typewriter. She still had three customers. One died last year, a count who owned a chateau in Normandy and a racing stable. His widow lives in Cannes and has never ordered any writing paper. There was also an embassy, but when the ambassador changed the new one ordered a different kind of paper.'

'There's still one customer?'

'There's still one customer, and that's why I said it's too easy. The customer's name is Émile Parendon, he's a lawyer, and he lives on Avenue Marigny. He's been using this paper for more than fifteen years and won't look at any other kind. Do you know the name?'

'Never heard of him. Has he ordered paper recently?'

'The last time was last October.'

'With a letterhead?'

'Yes, a very discreet one. Always a thousand sheets and a thousand envelopes.'

Maigret picked up the phone.

'Get me Maître Bouvier, please . . . The father.'

A lawyer he had known for more than twenty years, whose son was also a member of the bar.

'Hello, Bouvier? Maigret here. I hope I'm not disturbing you.'

'You? Never.'

'I'd like some information.'

'Confidential, of course.'

'Yes, just between ourselves. Are you familiar with a colleague of yours named Émile Parendon?'

Bouvier seemed surprised.

'What on earth could the Police Judiciaire possibly want with Parendon?'

'I don't know. Probably nothing.'

'It does seem unlikely. I've met Parendon five or six times in my life, no more than that. He almost never sets foot in the Palais de Justice and then only for civil cases.'

'How old is he?'

'Hard to say. He could be forty, he could just as easily be fifty.'

He must have turned to his secretary.

'My dear, can you look in the legal directory and find me the date of birth of Parendon . . . Émile. Actually, there is only one.'

Then, to Maigret:

'You must have heard of his father, who either is still alive or died just recently. Professor Parendon, a surgeon at Laennec, member of the Academy of Medicine, member of the Academy of Moral and Political Sciences, etcetera, etcetera. Quite a character! When I see you, I'll tell you all about him. He came to Paris very young from somewhere deep in the country. He was small and sturdy, like a young bull, and he didn't just *look* like a bull, if you get my meaning . . .'

'What about his son?'

'He's more of a jurist than anything else. He specializes in international law, especially maritime law. They say he's the top man in the field. People come from all over the world to consult him, and he's often asked to arbitrate in difficult cases with large sums of money at stake.'

'What kind of man is he?'

'Nondescript. I'm not sure I'd recognize him in the street.'

'Is he married?'

'Thank you, my dear . . . Here we are, I have his age. Forty-six . . . Is he married? I was going to say I couldn't remember, but now it's come back to me. Of course he's married. And not to just anybody! He married one of

Gassin de Beaulieu's daughters. You know Gassin de Beaulieu. He was one of the toughest magistrates at the time of the Liberation. Then he was appointed chief justice of the Court of Cassation. He's probably retired to his chateau in the Vendée. The family's very rich.'

'Do you know anything else?'

'What else do you expect me to know? I've never had to defend these people in court.'

'Do they go out a lot?'

'The Parendons? Not in the circles I mix in.'

'Thank you, my friend.'

'You owe me one . . .'

Maigret reread the letter, which Lapointe had placed on his desk. He read it twice, three times, and each time his face clouded over even more.

'You realize what all this means?'

'Yes, chief. It's going to land us in the shit. Sorry for the expression, but—'

'It's probably not strong enough. An eminent surgeon, a chief justice, a specialist in maritime law who lives on Avenue Marigny and uses the most expensive paper there is . . .'

The kind of clientele that Maigret feared the most. He already had the impression he was walking on eggshells.

'You think he's the one who wrote that—?'

'Him or someone from his household. Someone who has access to his writing paper, anyway.'

'It's strange, isn't it?'

Maigret, who was looking through the window, didn't reply. People who write anonymous letters are not generally in the habit of using their own writing paper, especially if it's of such rare quality.

'Well, can't be helped! I'll have to go and see him.'

He looked for the number in the phone book, then called on the direct line. A woman's voice replied:

'Maître Parendon's secretary.'

'Good morning, mademoiselle. This is Detective Chief Inspector Maigret of the Police Judiciaire. If it's not too much trouble, would it be possible for me to have a word with Maître Parendon?'

'One moment, please. I'll see.'

It couldn't have been easier. Almost immediately, a man's voice said:

'Parendon speaking.'

There was a questioning hint in the tone.

'I'd like to ask you, maître—'

'Who is this? My secretary didn't quite catch your name.'

'Detective Chief Inspector Maigret.'

'Now I understand why she was surprised. She must have understood what you said, but didn't imagine it could really be you. I'm very pleased to hear your voice, Monsieur Maigret. I've often thought about you. I've even occasionally been on the verge of writing to you to ask your opinion about certain matters. Knowing how busy you must be, I didn't dare.'

There was a shyness to Parendon's voice, and yet it was Maigret who was the more embarrassed of the two. He felt ridiculous now, with his meaningless letter.

'As you can see, I'm the one disturbing you. And what's

more, over a trifle. I'd prefer to talk to you about it in person, because I have a document to show you.'

'When would you like to do that?'

'Are you free at all this afternoon?'

'Would three thirty suit you? I confess I'm in the habit of taking a short nap and don't feel well when I miss it.'

'Three thirty would be fine. I'll come to your home. And thank you for your kind cooperation.'

'On the contrary, I'm delighted you're coming.'

When he hung up, he looked at Lapointe as if emerging from a dream.

'Did he seem surprised?'

'Not in the slightest. He didn't ask any questions. He's apparently delighted to make my acquaintance. Just one thing puzzles me. He claims he almost wrote to me several times to ask my opinion. But he doesn't deal with criminal cases, only civil ones. His speciality is the maritime code, about which I know absolutely nothing. Ask my opinion about what?'

Maigret cheated that day. He phoned his wife and told her he was detained at work. He felt like celebrating this spring sunshine by having lunch at the Brasserie Dauphine, where he even indulged himself in a pastis at the counter.

Maybe he was going to land in the shit, as Lapointe had said, but at least things were starting pleasantly enough.

Maigret had taken the bus as far as the Rond-Point des Champs-Élysées, then walked along Avenue Marigny, and in those hundred metres he did on foot he came across at least three faces he thought he recognized. He had forgotten that he was walking past the gardens of the Élysée and that the area was heavily guarded, day and night. The 'guardian angels' recognized him, too, and greeted him with discreet but respectful nods.

The building where Parendon lived was vast and solid, built to defy the centuries. The carriage entrance was flanked by bronze candelabra. Once through the archway, what came into view was not so much a concierge's lodge, more a veritable drawing room, with a table covered in green velvet, the kind you would find in a ministry.

Here, too, Maigret encountered a familiar face, a man named Lamule or Lamure, who had worked for a long time in the Sûreté.

He was wearing a grey uniform with silver buttons and seemed surprised to see Maigret loom up in front of him.

'Who have you come to see, chief?'

'Maître Parendon.'

'Lift or stairs on the left. It's on the first floor.'

There was a courtyard at the far end, with cars and garages and low buildings that must once have been stables. Maigret automatically knocked his pipe against his heel to empty it, then set off up the marble staircase.

When he rang at the only door, a butler in a white jacket opened it as if he had been listening out for him.

'Maître Parendon. I have an appointment.'

'This way, inspector.'

He took his hat from him without asking and admitted him to a library such as Maigret had never seen. The room was long and narrow, with a very high ceiling, and books entirely covered the walls, apart from the marble fireplace, on which stood the bust of a middle-aged man. All the books were bound, most of them in red. The only furniture consisted of a long table, two chairs and an armchair.

He would have liked to examine the titles of the volumes, but a young secretary in glasses was already advancing towards him.

'Will you follow me, inspector?'

Through windows that were more than three metres high, sunlight streamed in and played on the carpets, the furniture, the paintings. The corridor was filled with antique consoles, period furniture, busts and portraits of gentlemen in costumes of every period.

The young woman opened a light oak door and a man who had been sitting at his desk stood up and came to greet his visitor. He, too, was wearing glasses, with very thick lenses.

'Thank you, Mademoiselle Vague.'

There was a long way to walk, because this office was as vast as a reception room. Here, too, the walls were lined with books, as well as a few portraits, and the sun cast diamond-shaped patches of light on everything.

'If only you knew how happy I am to see you, Monsieur Maigret.'

He held out his hand, a small white hand that seemed boneless. By contrast with his surroundings, the man appeared even smaller than he probably was, short and frail and oddly light.

And yet he wasn't thin. If anything, he was quite rotund,

but the overall impression was that he lacked weight and substance.

'Come this way. Let's see, now, where would you prefer to sit?'

He indicated a fawn leather armchair near his desk.

'I think you'll be best here. I'm a little hard of hearing.'

Maigret's friend Bouvier had been right to say that Parendon's age was hard to pin down. On his face, in his blue eyes, there was still an almost childlike expression, and he looked at Maigret with a kind of awe.

'You can't imagine the number of times I've thought about you. When you're on a case, I devour several newspapers to make sure I don't miss anything. You could say I'm all agog to know how you'll proceed.'

Maigret felt awkward. Over the years, he had grown used to the curiosity of the public, but the enthusiasm of a man like Parendon put him in an embarrassing position.

'You know, I proceed the way anyone would if they were me.'

'Anyone perhaps. But there's no such thing as just anyone. It's a myth. What isn't a myth is the penal code, the magistrates, the jurors. And each juror, who the day before was just anyone, becomes a different person as soon as he enters a courtroom.'

He was dressed in dark grey, and the desk on which he was leaning with his elbows was much too large for him. All the same, he wasn't ridiculous. Nor, perhaps, was it innocence that made his pupils look so big behind the thick lenses of his glasses.

As a child at school, he might well have suffered from

being called a runt, but he had come to terms with it and now gave the impression of being a benevolent gnome who had to restrain his exuberance.

'May I ask you a personal question? How old were you when you started understanding people? I mean, understanding those we call criminals?'

Maigret blushed.

'I don't know,' he said hesitantly. 'I'm not even sure I do understand them.'

'Oh, but you do. And they know it. That's partly why they're almost relieved to confess.'

'It's the same with all my colleagues.'

'I could prove the contrary by reminding you of a number of cases, but that would bore you. You studied medicine, didn't you?'

'Only for two years.'

'From what I've read, your father died and as you were unable to pursue your studies, you joined the police.'

Maigret's position was increasingly delicate, almost ridiculous. He had come to ask questions and he was the one being questioned.

'I don't see two vocations in that switch, but a different way for the same personality to find fulfilment. Forgive me, I literally threw myself on you as soon as you arrived. I couldn't wait to see you. I'd have opened the door to you myself as soon as you rang the bell, but my wife wouldn't have liked that, she insists on a degree of decorum.'

He had lowered his voice to utter these last words. Now, pointing to a huge, almost life-size painting of a magistrate dressed in ermine, he whispered:

'My father-in-law.'

'Chief Justice Gassin de Beaulieu.'

'You know him?'

For a few moments, Parendon seemed so much like a little boy that Maigret thought it best to confess:

'I made inquiries before coming here.'

'Did you hear bad things about him?'

'Apparently, he's a great magistrate.'

'Oh, yes! A great magistrate! . . . Do you know the works of Henri Ey?'

'I've looked through his *Manual of Psychiatry*.'

'What about Sengès? Levy-Valensi? Maxwell?'

He pointed towards a section of the library where there were books bearing these names. They were all psychiatrists, none of whom had ever dealt with maritime law. Maigret recognized other names in passing that he had seen quoted in the bulletins of the International Society of Criminology, others whose works he had read: Lagache, Ruyssen, Genil-Perrin, and so on.

'Aren't you smoking?' his host asked suddenly in a surprised tone. 'I thought you always had your pipe in your mouth.'

'If you don't mind.'

'What can I offer you? My cognac isn't amazing, but I have a forty-year-old armagnac.'

He trotted over to a wall where a full panel between rows of books hid a drinks cabinet containing some twenty bottles as well as glasses of different sizes.

'Just a little, please.'

'My wife only allows me a drop on special occasions.

She says I have a fragile liver. According to her, everything in me is fragile, and I don't have a single solid organ.'

It amused him. He spoke of it without bitterness.

'Your good health! . . . The reason I've asked you these personal questions is that I'm fascinated by Article 64 of the Penal Code, which I'm sure you know better than I do.'

Maigret did indeed know it by heart. He had gone over it often enough in his head:

> There is no crime or offence if the accused was in a state of insanity at the time of the act, or if he was compelled by a force he was unable to resist.

'What do you think of it?' the gnome asked, leaning towards him.

'I've never wanted to be a magistrate. That way, I don't have to judge.'

'I'm glad to hear you say that. Faced with a guilty person in your office, or someone presumed guilty, are you able to determine to what extent he can be held responsible?'

'Not often. But then later, the psychiatrists—'

'This library is full of psychiatrists. The old ones, most of them, would say: "Yes, he's responsible," and go on their way with an easy conscience. But take another look at Henri Ey, for instance.'

'I know.'

'Do you speak English?'

'Yes, very badly.'

'You know what the English mean when they talk about a hobby?'

'Yes. A pastime, a pointless activity, an odd habit.'

'Well, my dear Monsieur Maigret, my hobby, my odd habit, as some say, is Article 64. And I'm not the only one. The French code isn't alone in having an article like this. There's something more or less identical in the United States, England, Germany, Italy . . .'

He was becoming animated. His face, rather pale earlier, was growing pink, and he was moving his chubby little hands about with unexpected energy.

'There are thousands of us in the world, no, tens of thousands, whose mission is to change that shameful Article 64, which is a remnant of bygone days. I'm not talking about a secret society. There are official groups in most countries, magazines, journals . . . Do you know what people say to us?'

And as if to personalize this *us*, he glanced at the portrait of his father-in-law.

'They say: "The Penal Code is a totality. If you change one stone, the whole edifice might well come crumbling down." Another objection is: "If you had your way, sentences would be left up to a doctor rather than a judge." I could talk about this for hours. I've written lots of articles on the subject. I'll take the liberty of getting my secretary to send you some. I'm sorry if that seems presumptuous of me. You know all about criminals, at first hand, if I can put it that way. As far as magistrates are concerned, they're people who fit into one or other category almost automatically. Do you follow me?'

'Yes.'

'Your good health.'

He caught his breath. He seemed surprised himself to have got so carried away.

'There aren't many people with whom I can have a heart-to-heart talk. I hope I haven't shocked you?'

'Not at all.'

'By the way, I haven't asked you why you wanted to see me. I was so delighted by this opportunity that it never even occurred to me to ask.'

He added ironically:

'I hope it's not about maritime law?'

Maigret had taken the letter from his pocket.

'I received this message in the post this morning. It isn't signed. I can't be certain that it came from here. I'd just like you to take a look at it.'

Curiously, as if he was particularly sensitive to touch, Parendon began by fingering the paper.

'It feels like mine. It's not easy to find. The last time I had to have it ordered from the manufacturer by my engraver.'

'That's the reason I'm here.'

Parendon had changed glasses and crossed his short legs, and was now moving his lips as he read, occasionally murmuring certain syllables:

. . . A murder will be committed soon, probably in a few days. Perhaps by someone I know, perhaps by myself . . .

He reread the paragraph carefully.

'It seems as if each word has been carefully chosen, doesn't it?'

'That's the impression I had, too.'

. . . In a way, it is inevitable . . .

'I don't like that phrase so much, it has something redundant about it.'

Then, handing the paper back to Maigret and again changing his glasses:

'Curious.'

He wasn't one for big words or bombast. *Curious.* That was his only comment.

'Something struck me,' Maigret said. 'Whoever wrote this letter doesn't call me inspector, as most people do, he or she uses my official title: detective chief inspector.'

'I noticed that, too. Have you placed the ad?'

'It'll be in *Le Monde* this evening and *Le Figaro* tomorrow morning.'

What was particularly strange was that Parendon wasn't surprised, or, if he was, he wasn't showing it. He was looking through the window at the gnarled trunk of a chestnut tree when his attention was drawn to a slight sound. He wasn't surprised by that either. Turning his head, he murmured:

'Come in, darling.'

And getting to his feet:

'Let me introduce Detective Chief Inspector Maigret in person.'

The woman was in her forties, elegant and vivacious, with extremely mobile eyes. It only took her a few seconds to examine Maigret from head to foot. If he'd had a little mud stain on his left shoe, she would probably have noticed.

'Pleased to meet you, inspector. I hope you're not here to arrest my husband? With his poor health, you'd be obliged to put him in the prison infirmary.'

There was nothing sharp about this. She wasn't saying it in any nasty way, but she was saying it all the same, with the most cheerful of smiles.

'I assume you're here for one of our servants?'

'I haven't received any complaint about them, and that would be a job for the local station anyway.'

She was clearly dying to know why he was there. Her husband sensed this, as did Maigret, but as if in a game neither of them made the slightest reference to it.

'What do you think of our armagnac?'

She had noticed the glasses.

'I hope you only had a drop, darling?'

She was wearing a light-coloured tailored suit, as if ready for spring.

'Well, gentlemen, I'll leave you to your business. I just wanted to tell you, darling, that I won't be back before eight. You can always reach me at Hortense's after seven.'

She didn't go out immediately. While the two men stood there in silence, she contrived to walk around the room, shifting an ashtray on a pedestal table, straightening a book.

'Goodbye, Monsieur Maigret. I'm delighted to have met you, believe me. You're an extremely interesting man.'

The door closed behind her. Parendon sat down again.

He waited another moment or two, as if the door were about to open again. At last he gave a childlike laugh.

'Did you hear that?'

Maigret didn't know what to say.

' "You're an extremely interesting man" . . . She hates it that you didn't tell her anything. Not only does she not know why you're here, but you didn't say anything about her dress, or above all, how young she looks. The greatest joy you could have given her would have been to take her for my daughter.'

'Do you have a daughter?'

'Yes, she's eighteen. She just passed her *baccalauréat* and is studying archaeology. I don't know how long that'll last. Last year, she wanted to be a laboratory assistant. I don't see much of her, except at mealtimes – when she condescends to eat with us. I have a son, too, Jacques. He's fifteen and is in his fourth year at the Lycée Racine. That's the whole family.'

He was speaking in a light tone, as if the words were of no importance or as if he were making fun of himself.

'Anyway, I'm wasting your time. Let's get back to your letter. Look, this is a sheet of my writing paper. I'm sure your experts will be able to tell you if it's the same paper, but I know in advance what they're going to find.'

He rang a bell and waited, turning towards the door.

'Mademoiselle Vague, would you be so kind as to bring me one of the envelopes we use for the suppliers?'

He explained:

'We pay our suppliers by cheque at the end of the month.

It would be pretentious to use the engraved envelopes when we send them payment. We have ordinary white envelopes for that.'

The young woman brought one.

'You'll be able to compare these two. If the envelope and paper match, you can be almost completely certain that the letter came from here.'

This did not seem to bother him unduly.

'Can you think of any reason why someone might have written that letter?'

He looked at Maigret, first with amazement, then with a slightly disappointed air.

'Any reason? I wasn't expecting that word, Monsieur Maigret. I understand that you had to ask the question. But why "reason"? I suppose everyone has one, wittingly or unwittingly.'

'Are there a lot of people living in this apartment?'

'Living day and night, not very many. My wife and I, of course.'

'Do you have separate bedrooms?'

Parendon gave him a very brief glance, as if Maigret had scored a point.

'How did you guess?'

'I don't know. I asked the question without thinking.'

'You're right, we do have separate bedrooms. My wife likes going to bed late and staying in bed in the mornings, whereas I'm an early riser. Feel free, by the way, to have a look around any of the rooms. I should tell you, before you start, that I didn't choose this place, or have anything to do with the furnishings. When my father-in-law' – a glance at the Chief Justice's portrait – 'retired to the Vendée, there was a kind of family council. There are four sisters, all of them married. We divided the inheritance in advance, so to speak, and my wife received this apartment with all its contents, including the portrait and the busts.'

He didn't laugh or smile as he said this. It was more subtle than that.

'One of her sisters will inherit the manor house in the Vendée, in the Forest of Vouvant, and the two others will divide up the securities. The Gassin de Beaulieus have been rich for a long time, so there'll be enough for everyone . . . What I'm saying is that this isn't really my home, but my father-in-law's, and only the books, the furniture in my bedroom and this office belong to me.'

'Your father is still alive, isn't he?'

'He lives almost opposite, in Rue de Miromesnil, in an apartment he's adapted for his old age. He's been a widower for thirty years. He used to be a surgeon.'

'A famous surgeon.'

'Ah, you know that, too. Then I'm sure you also know that *his* passion wasn't Article 64, but women. We used to have an apartment as huge as this, but much more modern, in Rue d'Aguesseau. My brother, who's a neurologist, lives there now with his wife . . . That's it as far as the family goes. I've already mentioned my daughter Paulette and her brother Jacques. By the way, if you want to be in her good books, you should know that my daughter likes to be called Bambi and insists on calling her brother Gus. I assume it'll pass. If it doesn't, well, it doesn't really matter . . . As for the domestic staff, as my wife would say, you've seen the butler, Ferdinand. His surname is Fauchois. He comes from the Berry, like my family. He isn't married. His room is at the far end of the courtyard, above the garages. Lise, the maid, sleeps in the apartment, and a woman named Madame Marchand comes in every day to clean. Oh, and I nearly forgot the cook, Madame Vauquin, whose husband is a pastry cook and who insists on going home at night . . . Aren't you taking notes?'

Maigret merely smiled, then got to his feet and walked over to an ashtray large enough to empty his pipe into it.

'Now for my side, if I can put it that way. You've seen Mademoiselle Vague. That's her real name, and she doesn't think it's ridiculous. I've always called my secretaries by their surnames. She never talks about her private life, and I'd have to check the files to find out her address. All I know is that she goes home by Métro and doesn't get upset if I ask her to stay late. She's about twenty-four or twenty-five, and she's seldom in a bad mood . . . To help me in my legal work, I have a very ambitious trainee named René Tortu. His office is at the end of the corridor. Last but not least, there's the one we call the scribe, a young man of about twenty who recently arrived from Switzerland and who has, I believe, ambitions to be a playwright. He does a bit of everything. A kind of office boy. When I'm entrusted with a case, and it's almost always a very big case, with millions at stake, even hundreds of millions, I have to work day and night for a week or several weeks. Then we go back to the old routine and I have time to . . .'

He blushed and smiled.

'. . . to think about our Article 64, Monsieur Maigret. One of these days, you really will have to tell me what you think of it. In the meantime, I'll give instructions to everyone to let you circulate as you see fit in the apartment and to answer your questions as honestly as possible.'

Maigret looked at him in some confusion, wondering if he was dealing with a skilful actor or, on the contrary, with a sickly little man who found consolation in a subtle sense of humour.

'I'll probably come back sometime tomorrow morning, but I shan't disturb you.'

'In that case, I'll probably disturb you.'

They shook hands, and it was almost a child's hand that Maigret held in his.

'Thank you for agreeing to see me, Monsieur Parendon.'

'Thank you for coming, Monsieur Maigret.'

Parendon trotted after him as far as the lift.

2.

He was back outside in the sun, with the smell of the first days of fine weather, a slight whiff of dust already in the air, the 'guardian angels' of the Élysée Palace walking about in a nonchalant manner and giving him discreet signs of recognition.

At the corner of the Rond-Point, an old woman was selling lilacs redolent of suburban gardens, and he had to resist the desire to buy some. What would he have looked like, arriving at headquarters with a cumbersome bunch of flowers?

He felt light, with a particular kind of lightness. He had just emerged from an unknown world in which he had felt less disoriented than he might have thought. As he walked along the street, rubbing shoulders with the other pedestrians, he saw again the solemn apartment, in which the shade of the great magistrate, who had probably given formal receptions there, still lingered.

From the first, as if to put him at his ease, Parendon had given him a kind of wink that meant:

'Don't let yourself be taken in. All this is a stage set. Even maritime law is just for show . . .'

And like a toy, he had produced his Article 64, the thing that interested him more than anything else in the world.

Unless Parendon was crafty? In any case, Maigret felt drawn to that sprightly gnome who couldn't take his eyes off him, as if he had never seen an inspector from the Police Judiciaire before.

He took advantage of the fine weather to walk down the Champs-Élysées as far as Place de la Concorde, where he finally took a bus. He couldn't find one with a platform, and he had to extinguish his pipe and sit inside.

It was the time for signing the correspondence at the Police Judiciaire, and it took him about twenty minutes to dispense with that. His wife was surprised to see him come home at six o'clock, looking quite cheerful.

'What's for dinner?'

'I was thinking of making—'

'Don't make anything. We're eating out.'

Anywhere as long as it was out. This wasn't a day like any other, and he was determined to keep it exceptional right to the end.

The days were getting longer. They found a restaurant in the Latin Quarter with a terrace surrounded by a glass partition and kept pleasantly warm by a brazier. The speciality was seafood, and Maigret chose a little of almost everything, including sea urchins that had been flown up from the South that same day.

His wife watched him with a smile.

'You look as if you had a good day.'

'I made the acquaintance of an odd character. An odd kind of apartment, too, with odd people . . .'

'Is it a murder?'

'I don't know. It hasn't been committed yet, but it could

happen any day now. And if it does, I'll find myself in a pretty tricky situation.'

He seldom talked to her about cases in progress, and she usually learned about them more from the newspapers and the radio than through her husband. This time, he couldn't resist the desire to show her the letter.

'Read this.'

They were on the dessert course. With the grilled mullet, they had drunk a Pouilly fumé, and the smell of it still lingered in the air. Madame Maigret gave him a look of surprise as she handed him back the letter.

'Was it a child?' she asked.

'There is a young boy in the house. I haven't seen him yet. But not all children are young. Some are quite mature, some are even old.'

'Do you think it's for real?'

'Someone wanted me to visit that apartment. Otherwise he wouldn't have used writing paper that can only be found in two stationery shops in Paris.'

'If he's planning to commit a murder—'

'He doesn't say he's going to commit a murder. He says there's going to be one, but he doesn't seem too sure who the murderer will be.'

For once, she didn't take him seriously.

'You'll see, it's a hoax.'

He paid the bill. It was so mild that they walked home, making a detour via Ile Saint-Louis.

He found lilacs in Rue Saint-Antoine, so there ended up being some in the apartment that night after all.

The following morning, the sun was as bright and the

air as transparent, but already people weren't paying as much attention to it. He again gathered Lucas, Janvier and Lapointe for the little briefing and immediately looked for the letter in the pile of mail.

He wasn't sure he would find it because the ad in *Le Monde* hadn't appeared until mid-afternoon on the previous day and it had only just been published in *Le Figaro*.

'Here it is!' he said, waving it.

The same envelope, the same carefully traced block capitals, the same writing paper with the letterhead cut off.

He was no longer addressed as 'Detective Chief Inspector', and the tone had changed.

You were wrong, Monsieur Maigret, to come before you received my second letter. It has got them all stirred up, and that may well bring things forward. The murder may be committed any time now, and it will be partly your fault.

I thought you were more patient, more cautious. Do you really imagine you can discover the secrets of a household in one afternoon?

You are more credulous and perhaps more vain than I had thought. I cannot help you any longer. All I advise is that you continue your inquiries without giving credence to what anybody tells you.

I wish you all the best. In spite of everything, I still admire you.

The three men could all see how embarrassed he was and how reluctant to show them the letter. They were even more embarrassed than he was at the casual way in which the anonymous writer treated their chief.

'Couldn't it be a child playing games?'

'That's what my wife said last night.'

'What do you think?'

'I don't agree.'

No, he didn't think this was a hoax. And yet there was nothing tragic about the atmosphere of the apartment on Avenue Marigny. Everything there was bright and neat. The butler had welcomed him with calm dignity. The secretary with the funny name was lively and friendly. As for Parendon, in spite of his strange physique, he had been quite a cheerful host.

The idea of a hoax hadn't occurred to Parendon either. He hadn't objected to this intrusion into his private life. He had spoken a lot, about different subjects, especially about Article 64, but, deep down, had there been a kind of latent anxiety?

Maigret didn't mention it during the daily briefing. He knew that his colleagues would shrug their shoulders at the sight of him involving himself in such a bizarre affair.

'Anything new in your department, Maigret?'

'Janvier's about to arrest the man who murdered the postmistress. We're almost certain it's him, but we thought it was best to wait and find out if he had an accomplice. The young woman who lives with him is pregnant . . .'

All humdrum, everyday stuff. An hour later, he left the everyday behind on entering the building on Avenue Marigny, where the uniformed concierge waved to him through the glass door of the lodge.

The butler, Ferdinand, asked as he took his hat:

'Would you like me to tell monsieur you're here?'

'No. Take me to the secretary's office.'

Mademoiselle Vague! That was it! He remembered her name. She occupied a small room lined with green-painted filing cabinets and was typing on an electric typewriter of the latest model.

'Is it me you want to see?' she asked, quite unflustered.

She stood up, looked around her and pointed to a chair near the window that looked out on the courtyard.

'Unfortunately, I don't have an armchair for you. If you'd rather, we could go to the library or the drawing room.'

'I'd rather stay here.'

From somewhere, a vacuum cleaner could be heard. Another typewriter was clattering in one of the offices. A man's voice, not Parendon's, was talking on the phone:

'Yes, of course . . . I understand perfectly well, my dear friend, but the law is the law, even if it sometimes goes against common sense . . . Of course I talked to him about it . . . No, he doesn't want to see you today or tomorrow, and besides, there'd be no point.'

'Monsieur Tortu?' Maigret asked.

She nodded. Yes, it was the trainee they could hear speaking like this in the next room, and Mademoiselle Vague went and closed the door, cutting the sound off as if turning the dial of a radio.

The window was still half open and a chauffeur in blue overalls was hosing down a Rolls-Royce.

'Does that one belong to Monsieur Parendon?'

'No, the tenants on the second floor. They're from Peru.'

'Does Monsieur Parendon have a chauffeur?'

'He has to. His sight isn't good enough to allow him to drive.'

'Which car?'

'The Cadillac. Madame uses it more than he does, although she also has a little English car . . . Is the noise bothering you? Would you rather I closed the window?'

No. The jet of water was all part of the atmosphere, along with the spring weather and the kind of building he was now in.

'Do you know why I'm here?'

'All I know is that we're all at your disposal and that we have to answer your questions, even if we find them too personal.'

Once again, he took the first letter from his pocket. He had better have it photocopied when he got back to Quai des Orfèvres, or it would end up no more than a piece of scrap paper.

As she read it, he examined her face. Her round horn-rimmed glasses didn't detract from her looks. She wasn't beautiful in the usual sense of the word, but she was pleasant. Her mouth was particularly striking, the lips full, the corners turned up in a smile.

'And . . . ?' she said, giving him back the letter.

'What do you think?'

'What does Monsieur Parendon think?'

'The same as you.'

'What do you mean?'

'That he was no more surprised by it than you seem to be.'

She made an effort to smile, but it was clear that the blow had struck home.

'Should I have reacted differently?'

'When it's announced that a murder is going to be committed in a household . . .'

'It can happen in any household, can't it? Before a man becomes a criminal, I assume he behaves like any other man, *is* like any other man, otherwise . . .'

'Otherwise we'd arrest all future murderers in advance. You're right.'

The strangest thing was that she had thought of this, because few people, in the course of his long career, had expressed this idea, simple as it was, to Maigret.

'I had the ad put in. This morning I received a second letter.'

He handed it to her, and she read it with the same attention, but this time with an added touch of anxiety.

'I'm starting to understand,' she murmured.

'What?'

'Why you're worried and why you're taking personal charge of the investigation.'

'Do you mind if I smoke?'

'Go ahead. I'm allowed to smoke here, too, which isn't the case in most offices.'

She lit a cigarette simply, without any of the flourishes that so many women affect. She smoked to relax. She sat back a little in her swivel chair. The office wasn't like a normal commercial office. Although the table for the typewriter was made of metal, there was a very beautiful Louis XIII table right beside it.

'Is Monsieur Parendon's son the kind of boy who plays practical jokes?'

'Gus? Quite the opposite. He's intelligent, but reserved. At school, he's always top of the class, even though he never studies.'

'What are his interests?'

'Music and electronics. He's installed a sophisticated hi-fi system in his room and he subscribes to all kinds of science magazines. Look, here's one that arrived in the post this morning. *Tomorrow's Electronics*. It's up to me to take them to his room.'

'Does he go out a lot?'

'I'm not here in the evenings, but I don't think so.'

'Does he have friends?'

'Sometimes a classmate of his comes to listen to records or help him with experiments.'

'How well does he get on with his father?'

She seemed surprised by the question. She thought about it, then smiled apologetically.

'I don't know how to answer that. I've been working for Monsieur Parendon for five years. This is only my second position in Paris.'

'What was the first?'

'I worked in a commercial firm in Rue Réaumur. I was unhappy because the work didn't interest me.'

'Who brought you here?'

'It was René – I mean Monsieur Tortu – who told me about this job.'

'Did you know him well?'

'We used to have dinner in the same restaurant in Rue Caulaincourt.'

'Do you live in Montmartre?'

'Yes, on Place Constantin-Pecqueur.'

'Was Tortu your boyfriend?'

'He's nearly one metre eighty tall, for a start . . . Then, except for one occasion, there was never anything between us.'

'Except for one occasion?'

'I have instructions to be completely honest, don't I? . . . One evening, not long before I started here, we went to the cinema in Place Clichy after leaving Chez Maurice . . . Chez Maurice is our restaurant in Rue Caulaincourt.'

'Do you always eat there?'

'Almost every evening. I'm part of the furniture.'

'What about him?'

'Not so often since he got engaged.'

'So, after the cinema . . .'

'He asked if he could come back to my place for a nightcap . . . We'd already had a few, and I was a little drunk . . . I refused, because I hate men coming into my apartment . . . It's physical . . . I preferred to go with him to his place in Rue des Saules.'

'Why didn't you ever go back?'

'Because it didn't work out. We both felt it . . . A matter of chemistry, when you come down to it . . . We've remained good friends.'

'Is he getting married soon?'

'I don't think he's in any hurry.'

'Is his fiancée also a secretary?'

'She's the assistant to Dr Parendon, my boss's brother.'

Maigret was puffing at his pipe, trying to absorb all these people he hadn't known the day before but who had suddenly appeared in his life.

'As we were on the subject, I'm going to ask you another personal question. Are you sleeping with Monsieur Parendon?'

It was very much her manner. She listened attentively to the question, her face solemn, paused for a moment then, as she replied, began to smile, with a smile that was both wicked and spontaneous, while her eyes sparkled behind her glasses.

'In a way, the answer is yes. We do sometimes make love, but it's always on the sly. The word "sleep" isn't really appropriate. We've never slept side by side.'

'Does Tortu know?'

'We've never talked about it, but he probably suspects.'

'Why?'

'When you're more familiar with the apartment, you'll understand. Let's see, how many people come and go during the day? Monsieur and Madame Parendon, plus their two children, that makes four. Three in the office, that makes seven. Ferdinand, the cook, the maid and the housekeeper bring us to eleven. And I haven't mentioned madame's masseur, who comes four mornings a week, or her sisters, or mademoiselle's friends. There may be a lot of rooms, but we always end up running into each other. Especially here.'

'Why here?'

'Because everyone comes to this office to get their supplies of paper, stamps, paper clips. If Gus needs a piece of string, he looks in these drawers. Bambi always needs stamps or adhesive tape. As for madame . . .'

He looked at her, curious as to what she would say next.

'She's everywhere. True, she goes out a lot, but you never know if she's out or in. You'll have noticed that all the corridors and most of the rooms are carpeted. You don't hear anyone coming. The door opens, and you see someone you weren't expecting. Sometimes, for instance, she opens my door and says, "Oh, I'm sorry!" as if she's made a mistake.'

'You mean she's nosy?'

'That or absent-minded. Unless it's just a habit.'

'Has she ever caught you with her husband?'

'I'm not sure. Once, just before Christmas, when we thought she was at her hairdresser's, she did come in at a rather delicate moment. We had time to compose ourselves, at least I think we did, but I can't be certain. She seemed perfectly natural and started talking to her husband about the gift she'd just bought for Gus.'

'Did her attitude towards you change?'

'No. She's pleasant to everyone, in her own special way, rather as if she's hovering over us to protect us. In my own head, I sometimes call her *the angel*.'

'But you don't like her?'

'I wouldn't have her as my friend, if that's what you mean.'

A bell rang, and the young woman sprang to her feet.

'Will you excuse me? The boss is calling.'

She was already at the door, having grabbed a stenographer's pad and a pencil in passing.

Maigret stayed where he was, looking out at the courtyard, still in shadow, where the chauffeur was now polishing the Rolls with a chamois leather and whistling a tune.

Mademoiselle Vague hadn't come back, and Maigret remained in his seat by the window. He wasn't impatient, even though he usually hated to wait. He could have taken a walk along the corridor, to the office occupied by Tortu and Julien Baud, but it was as if he was numb, his eyes half closed, looking now at one object, now at another.

The table that served as a desk had heavy oak feet with sober carvings and must once have been in another room. The surface had been polished by time. On it was a beige blotting pad with four leather corners. The pencil box was a very ordinary plastic one, and contained pens, pencils, a rubber and a scalpel. There was a dictionary near the typewriter table.

After a while, he frowned, stood up as if reluctantly and walked over to the table to get a closer look at it. He hadn't been mistaken. A thin, still fresh groove ran across the surface, such as might have been made by the scalpel in cutting a sheet of paper.

Next to the pencil box was a flat metal ruler.

'You noticed it, too?'

He gave a start. Mademoiselle Vague had come back in, the stenographer's pad still in her hand.

'What are you talking about?'

'The groove. Isn't it terrible to ruin such a beautiful table?'

'Do you know who did it?'

'It could have been anybody with access to this room, in other words, anybody. As I told you, they all just make themselves at home.'

So he wouldn't have to search. The previous day, he had vowed to examine all the tables in the apartment, having noticed that the paper had been cut neatly, as if with a guillotine.

'If you don't mind, Monsieur Parendon would like to see you for a moment . . .'

Maigret noticed that there was nothing written on the pad.

'Did you tell him about our conversation?'

She replied without any embarrassment:

'Yes.'

'Including what was said about your relationship?'

'Of course.'

'Is that why he called you?'

'No. He really did have something to ask me about the case he's working on.'

'I'll be back to see you in a moment. I don't suppose you need to take me there again?'

She smiled.

'He told you to come and go as if this was your home, didn't he?'

He knocked at the tall oak door and opened it to find the little man at his vast desk, which this morning was covered with official-looking papers.

43

'Come in, Monsieur Maigret. I'm sorry to have interrupted you. Actually, I didn't know you were with my secretary. So, you're starting to find out a little bit more about our household. Would it be indiscreet of me to ask if I could take a glance at the second letter?'

Maigret willingly handed it to him. He had the impression that the man's face, already colourless, became waxy. His blue eyes no longer sparkled behind the thick lenses of the glasses but turned to fix Maigret with an anxious, questioning stare.

' "The murder may be committed any time now" . . . Do you believe that?'

Maigret, who was looking at him just as fixedly, merely replied:

'Do you?'

'I don't know. I don't know anything any more. Yesterday, I was inclined to take the whole matter lightly. I didn't think it was a hoax, but I was tempted to think that someone was taking an innocent, if underhand, kind of revenge.'

'Revenge on whom?'

'Me, my wife, anyone here. A clever way to bring the police in and have us subjected to questioning.'

'Have you talked about it to your wife?'

'I had to, after she saw you in my office.'

'You could have told her I'd come to see you on a professional matter.'

Parendon's face expressed mild surprise.

'Would Madame Maigret be content with an explanation like that?'

'My wife never asks me questions.'

'Mine does. And she repeats them, just as you do in your interrogations, if the newspapers are to be believed, until she feels she's got to the bottom of things. Then, as far as possible, she confirms it with apparently innocuous little questions addressed to Ferdinand, the cook, my secretary or the children.'

He wasn't complaining. There was no sourness in his voice. Rather a kind of admiration, when it came down to it. He seemed to be talking about a phenomenon that deserved praise.

'What was her reaction?'

'That it's a servant taking revenge.'

'Do they have grounds for complaint?'

'They always have a reason to complain. Madame Vauquin, the cook, for example, whenever we have a dinner party, works quite late, whereas the cleaner, whatever happens, leaves at six. On the other hand, the cleaner earns two hundred francs less. Do you see what I mean?'

'What about Ferdinand?'

'Would you believe that Ferdinand, who's so stiff and correct, is a former legionnaire who used to take part in commando operations? Nobody checks what he does in his room over the garage in the evenings, who comes to see him, where he goes.'

'Do you agree with your wife?'

After a moment's hesitation, Parendon made up his mind to be honest.

'No.'

'Why not?'

'Because none of them would have written the phrases found in these letters or used certain words.'

'Are there any weapons in the house?'

'My wife owns two hunting rifles, because she's often invited on hunts. I don't shoot.'

'Because of your eyesight?'

'Because I hate killing animals.'

'Do you own a gun?'

'Yes, an old Browning, which I keep in a drawer in my bedside table. A habit a lot of people have, I think. You tell yourself that if ever a burglar . . .'

He laughed softly.

'I could at least scare them. Here, look.'

He opened a drawer in his desk and took out a box of cartridges.

'The automatic is in my room, at the other end of the apartment, and the cartridges are here, a habit I got into when the children were younger and I was afraid of an accident. Come to think of it, they're old enough now, so I could load my Browning.'

He continued to rummage in the drawer and this time took out an American-style cosh.

'You know where this toy comes from? Three years ago, I was surprised to be summoned to the police station. When I got there, I was asked if I had a son named Jacques. He was twelve at the time. A fight had broken out between boys outside the school, and the constable had found Gus in possession of this cosh. I questioned him when he got home and found out that he'd got it from a chum of his in return for six packets of chewing-gum!'

He smiled, amused by this memory.

'Does he have violent tendencies?'

'He went through a difficult period when he was about twelve or thirteen. He'd fly into brief but violent tempers, especially when his sister made some kind of remark. That's all over now. These days, he's a bit too calm, too solitary for my taste.'

'Does he have any friends?'

'I only know of one, who comes to see him quite often. They listen to music together. The boy's name is Génuvier, his father owns a patisserie on Faubourg Saint-Honoré. You probably know the name. Women come from far and wide for his cakes.'

'If you don't mind, I'm going back to speak to your secretary.'

'What do you think of her?'

'She seems intelligent. She's spontaneous and at the same time thoughtful.'

That seemed to please Parendon, who purred:

'She's very precious to me.'

He plunged back into his files, and Maigret went back to Mademoiselle Vague's office. She was making no pretence of working and was conspicuously waiting for him.

'I have a question you may find ridiculous, mademoiselle. Has Monsieur Parendon's son—'

'Everyone calls him Gus.'

'Fine! Has Gus ever flirted with you?'

'He's only fifteen.'

'I know. That's precisely the age when boys feel curious about things, or even develop crushes.'

She thought this over. Like Parendon, she took time to think before replying, as if he had taught her precision.

'No,' she said at last. 'When I met him, he was a little boy who came and asked me for stamps for his collection and filched an incredible number of pencils and rolls of adhesive tape. Occasionally, he'd ask me to help him with his homework. He'd sit where you are and watch me working with a solemn look on his face.'

'And now?'

'Now he's half a head taller than me and has been shaving for a year. The only thing he ever filches from me is cigarettes, when he's forgotten to buy them.'

And with that, she lit one, while Maigret slowly filled his pipe.

'Does he come to see you more frequently now?'

'On the contrary. As I think I told you, he has his own life, outside the family, apart from mealtimes. And even then he refuses to come to the table when there are guests and prefers to eat in the kitchen.'

'Does he get on well with the staff?'

'He doesn't make any distinction between people. Even when he's late, he won't allow the chauffeur to drive him to school, for fear of being seen in a limousine by his classmates.'

'In other words, he's ashamed of living in a place like this?'

'Something like that, yes.'

'Have his relations with his sister improved?'

'Don't forget, I don't eat my meals with them and don't often see them together. I think he looks at her as some kind of curious creature, trying to figure out what makes her tick, rather as he might look at an insect.'

'What about his mother?'

'She's a little boisterous for him. I mean, she's always bustling about, always talking about lots of people.'

'I see . . . And what about the girl? Paulette, if I remember correctly.'

'They all call her Bambi. Don't forget, both children have nicknames. Gus and Bambi. I don't know what they call me among themselves – it must be something quite funny.'

'How does Bambi get on with her mother?'

'Not well.'

'Do they argue?'

'Oh, no, they barely talk to each other.'

'Who does the animosity come from?'

'From Bambi. You'll see her. Young as she is, she judges the people around her, and you can tell from the way she looks at them that she judges them harshly.'

'Unfairly?'

'Not always.'

'Does she get on well with you?'

'She accepts me.'

'Does she sometimes come and see you in your office?'

'When she needs me to type up one of her lessons or photocopy a document.'

'Does she ever talk to you about her friends?'

'No, never.'

'Do you have the impression she knows about your relationship with her father?'

'I've sometimes wondered that. I don't know. Anyone could have caught us without our knowing.'

'Does she love her father?'

'She's taken him under her wing. She probably thinks he's victimized by her mother, which is why she resents her mother for always being at the centre of things.'

'In other words, Monsieur Parendon doesn't play a major role in the family?'

'Not a conspicuous one, no.'

'Has he ever tried?'

'In the past, perhaps, before I came here. He must have realized it was a losing battle and . . .'

'. . . and withdrew into his shell.'

She laughed.

'Not as much as you think. He knows what's going on. He doesn't ask questions like Madame Parendon. But he listens, he observes, he deduces. He's an extremely intelligent man.'

'That's the impression I had, too.'

She seemed delighted by this. There was a friendlier look in her eyes now, as if he had won her over. He had grasped the fact that she sometimes slept with Parendon not because he was her boss but because she had real feelings for him.

'I'd wager you don't have a boyfriend.'

'That's true. I don't want one.'

'Doesn't it bother you to live alone?'

'On the contrary. It's having someone around me I wouldn't be able to bear. Especially having someone in my bed.'

'Never any flings?'

Again that slight hesitation between truth and false-hood.

'Occasionally . . . Not very often.'

And with comical pride, she added, as if it were a profession of faith:

'But never at my place.'

'How do Gus and his father get on? I asked the question earlier but the conversation got diverted.'

'Gus admires him. But he admires him from a distance, without showing it, with a kind of humility . . . Really, to understand this family, you'd have to get to know them, and your investigation would never end. As you know, the apartment used to belong to Monsieur Gassin de Beaulieu and it's still full of memories of him. For the past three years, he's been disabled and hasn't left his manor house in the Vendée. But, before that, he'd often come and spend a week here – he still has his room. As soon as he arrived, he'd be the master of the house again.'

'So you knew him?'

'Very well. He used to dictate all his mail to me.'

'What kind of man is he? Judging from his portrait—'

'The one in Monsieur Parendon's office? If you've seen the portrait, you've seen him. He's the kind of magistrate they call upright and learned. You know what I mean? An important figure who always walked around looking larger than life, as if he'd just come down off his pedestal. Whenever he stayed here, we weren't allowed to make any noise. We all walked on tiptoe and whispered. The children, who of course were younger then, lived in terror . . . Monsieur Parendon's father, on the other hand, the surgeon . . .'

'Does he still visit?'

'Not very often. That's what I was going to tell you. You know his story, everyone does. He's the son of peasants from the Berry, and he's always behaved like a peasant, deliberately using colourful language, even in his classes. Just a few years ago, he was still a force of nature. As he lives not far from here, in Rue de Miromesnil, he'd often drop by, and the children loved him. Not everyone liked that.'

'Especially not Madame Parendon.'

'There definitely wasn't any love lost between them. I don't know anything specific. The servants mentioned a violent scene that took place. Whatever happened, he doesn't come here any more and his son goes to see him every two or three days.'

'In other words, the Gassins have won out against the Parendons.'

'More than you think . . .'

The air was blue with smoke, both from Maigret's pipe and from Mademoiselle Vague's cigarettes. She went to the window and opened it a little more to clear the air.

'The children also have all the aunts and uncles and cousins to deal with,' she continued in an amused tone. 'Monsieur Gassin de Beaulieu had four daughters, and the other three also live in Paris. They have children ranging from ten to twenty-two. Incidentally, last spring one of the girls married an officer who works at the Ministry of the Navy . . . That's the Gassin de Beaulieus . . . If you like, I can make you a list, with the names of the husbands . . .'

'I don't think that'll be necessary at this stage. Do they come here often?'

'One or other of them, every now and again. Although they all made good marriages, as they say, they still consider this apartment the family home.'

'Whereas . . .'

'You know what I'm getting at before I say it. Monsieur Parendon's brother, Germain, is a doctor specializing in paediatric neurology. He's married to a former actress who's still young and lively.'

'Does he look like . . .'

Maigret was a little embarrassed by his question.

She understood. 'No, he's as broad and strong as his father, and much taller. He's a very handsome man, and surprisingly gentle. He and his wife don't have any children. They don't go out much and only see a few close friends.'

'But they don't come here.'

Maigret sighed: he was starting to get a fairly clear picture of the family.

'Monsieur Parendon goes to see them on the evenings when his wife has a bridge party, because he hates cards. Every now and again, Monsieur Germain comes and keeps him company in the office. I know it when I arrive in the morning because the room smells of cigars.'

It was as if Maigret suddenly changed tone. He didn't become threatening, or stern, but there was no trace now of banter or amusement in his voice or his eyes.

'Listen to me, Mademoiselle Vague. I'm convinced that you've answered me with complete honesty, and you've even sometimes anticipated my questions. I have one more question to ask you and I'd like you to be just as honest. Do you think those letters are a hoax?'

She replied without hesitation:

'No.'

'Before they were written, had you already sensed that something dramatic was brewing in the apartment?'

Now she took her time, lighting another cigarette.

'Perhaps.'

'When?'

'I don't know. I'm trying to think. Perhaps after the holidays . . . Around that time anyway . . .'

'What did you notice?'

'Nothing in particular. It was in the air. A kind of suffocation, I'd be tempted to say.'

'In your opinion, who's the person under threat?'

She abruptly turned red and said nothing.

'Why don't you answer?'

'Because you know perfectly well what I'm going to say: Monsieur Parendon.'

He stood up with a sigh.

'Thank you. I think I've tortured you enough this morning. It's quite likely I'll be back to see you soon.'

'Are you going to question the others?'

'Not before lunch. It's almost midday. Later, probably.'

She watched him leave – big, heavy, clumsy-looking – then, abruptly, when the front door had closed, she started crying.

3.

In Rue de Miromesnil, there was a relic of the old days, a dimly lit little restaurant where the menu was still written on a slate and where you caught a glimpse of the owner's wife through a glass door, a huge woman with legs like columns, officiating at her oven.

The regulars had their serviettes in pigeonholes and scowled when they found their seats occupied. This didn't often happen, because the waitress, Emma, didn't like new faces. The place was frequented by a number of veteran inspectors from the Sûreté, as well as clerks of a kind you seldom saw any more, whom you could well imagine in black oversleeves at ancient black desks.

The owner, who was at the counter, recognized Maigret and came out to greet him.

'Haven't seen you around here for a while. Well, you always did have a good nose. We have andouillette today.'

Every now and again, Maigret liked to eat alone like this, letting his gaze wander over an old-fashioned setting and people who worked mostly in the kind of courtyards where you found unlikely offices, small-time lawyers, pawnbrokers, orthopaedists, stamp dealers and so on.

As he liked to say, he wasn't thinking, he was ruminating. His mind roamed from one thought to the next, one image to the next, sometimes mixing old cases in with the current one.

Parendon fascinated him. In his mind, as he ate the crisp, juicy andouillette, with its accompaniment of *frites* that didn't smell of burned fat, the gnome took on a now touching, now alarming aspect.

'Article 64, Monsieur Maigret! Don't forget 64!'

Was it really an obsession? Why was this business lawyer, whom people came from far and wide, at great expense, to consult on all matters maritime, so mesmerized by the only article in the Code that actually dealt with human responsibility?

Very cautiously, of course. Without giving the slightest definition of insanity. And limiting it to the moment of the act, in other words, the moment when the crime was committed.

He knew a few veteran psychiatrists, the kind judges were happy to have as expert witnesses because they didn't go in for subtleties.

The only things they knew that could limit a criminal's responsibility were lesions or malformations of the brain, plus – since the Penal Code mentioned it in the following article – epilepsy.

But how to establish that a man, at the moment he killed another man, at the exact instant of the homicidal act, was in complete possession of his faculties, let alone state that he was capable of resisting his impulse?

Article 64, yes . . . Maigret had often discussed it, especially with his old friend Pardon. It was also discussed at almost every congress of the International Society of

Criminology, and there were thick volumes on the subject – the very volumes that filled most of Parendon's bookshelves.

'Well? Do you like it?'

The jovial owner refilled his glass with a Beaujolais that was perhaps a little young but ideally fruity.

'Your wife hasn't lost her touch.'

'She'll be happy if you tell her that before you leave.'

The apartment on Avenue Marigny was very much in the image of Gassin de Beaulieu, a man used to ermine, a commander of the Legion of Honour, a man who had never had any doubts about the Code, the law or himself.

Around Maigret sat thin men, fat men, men of thirty and men of fifty. Almost all of them were eating alone, staring into space or at a page of a newspaper, and they all had in common that particular patina caused by a humble, monotonous life.

We have a tendency to imagine people the way we would like them to be. In point of fact, one had a crooked nose or a receding chin, another drooping shoulders, while his neighbour was obese. Half of them were balding and at least half wore glasses.

Why was Maigret thinking about this? No reason. Because Parendon, in his vast office, looked like a gnome – some would have said, more cruelly, a monkey.

As for Madame Parendon . . . He had barely seen her. She had put in only a brief appearance, as if to provide him with a glimpse of her brilliant personality. How had she and her husband met? Was it a chance meeting or the result of a family arrangement?

Between the two of them, there was Gus, who played music on his hi-fi and experimented on electronics in his room with a boy whose father owned a patisserie. He was taller and stronger than his father, fortunately, and if Mademoiselle Vague was to be believed, he was a well-adjusted young man.

There was also his sister, Bambi, who was studying archaeology. Did she really plan to spend her life digging in the deserts of the Near East, or were her studies nothing but an alibi?

Mademoiselle Vague was fierce in her defence of her boss, even though she was only ever able to make love to him on the sly, in a corner of the office.

Why didn't they arrange to meet somewhere else, for heaven's sake? Were they both so afraid of Madame Parendon? Or else was it through a sense of guilt that they insisted on giving their relations this furtive, impromptu character?

There were also the ex-legionnaire who'd become a butler, and the cook and the cleaner who hated each other because of working hours and wages. There was a maid named Lise, whom Maigret didn't know and whom nobody had said much about.

There was René Tortu, who had slept just once with Mademoiselle Vague and who was dragging out his engagement to another woman, and finally the Swiss, Julien Baud, who was taking his first steps in Paris as a pen-pusher while dreaming of a life in the theatre.

Which side was each of these individuals on? The Gassins' or the Parendons'?

In all this, someone wanted to kill someone else.

And, downstairs, almost ironically, a former Sûreté inspector was working as a concierge!

Opposite, the gardens of the Elysée Palace and, through the trees that were starting to turn prematurely green, the famous steps where the president was always being photographed shaking hands with important guests.

Wasn't there a certain inconsistency? The bistro around Maigret seemed more real, more solid. It was everyday life. People of modest means, of course, but they outnumber the rest, even if they are less noticeable, even if they dress in dark clothes, speak less loudly, keep close to the walls or crowd together in the Métro . . .

Without asking for it, he was served a rum baba smothered in whipped cream, another speciality of the owner's wife. Maigret made sure he went and shook her hand in the kitchen. He even had to kiss her on both cheeks. It was tradition.

'I hope you won't stay away so long next time?'

If the murderer took his time, there was a good chance Maigret would be back here often . . .

Yes, he was again thinking about the murderer. The murderer who wasn't yet one. The potential murderer.

Aren't there thousands and thousands of potential murderers in Paris?

Why did this one feel the need to alert Maigret in advance? Was it a kind of romanticism? Was it to make himself interesting? To have Maigret testify for him eventually? Or else was it because he wanted to be stopped?

Stopped how?

Once out in the sun, Maigret walked as far as Saint-Philippe-du-Roule and turned left, stopping occasionally to look in a shop window: very expensive, often pointless things that nevertheless got sold.

He passed Roman's Stationers, where he was amused to read double-barrelled names from the upper classes on business cards or engraved invitations. It was here that the writing paper that had started everything had come from. Without those anonymous letters, Maigret would never have heard of the Parendons, the Gassin de Beaulieus, the aunts and uncles and cousins.

Like him, other people were walking the streets for the pleasure of blinking in the sun and breathing in blasts of warm air. He felt like shrugging his shoulders, jumping on the first bus with a platform and going back to headquarters.

'To hell with the Parendons!'

There, he might find some poor loser who had killed someone because he couldn't stand it any more, or some young Pigalle tearaway who'd moved to Paris from Marseille or Bastia and had shot down a rival to show that he was a man.

He sat down on a café terrace, near a brazier, and had a coffee. Then he went inside and shut himself in the phone booth.

'Maigret here. Put me through to someone from my office, please . . . It doesn't matter . . . Janvier, Lucas or Lapointe preferably.'

It was Lapointe who answered.

'Anything new, son?'

'A phone call from Madame Parendon. She wanted to speak to you personally, and I had a hard time getting her to understand that you had lunch like anyone else.'

'What did she want?'

'She wanted you to go and see her as soon as possible.'

'At home?'

'Yes. She'll wait for you until four. After that, she has an important appointment.'

'Probably with her hairdresser. Anything else?'

'Yes. But this other thing may be a joke. Half an hour ago, the switchboard operator took a call from someone, she wasn't sure if it was a man or a woman, the voice was odd, it might have been a child. Anyway, the person was panting, either because they were in a hurry or they were upset, and said very quickly, "Tell Inspector Maigret to hurry up." The switchboard operator didn't have time to ask any questions, they'd already hung up. This time, it's not a letter, which makes me wonder . . .'

Maigret almost said:

'Don't.'

He wasn't wondering anything, wasn't trying to play guessing games. All the same, he was worried.

'Thanks a lot, son. I'm going back to Avenue Marigny now. If there's anything new, I can be reached there.'

The fingerprints on the two letters hadn't produced any results. For years now, compromising prints had been becoming increasingly rare. They had been mentioned so often in newspapers, in novels, on television, that even the dumbest criminals took precautions.

He passed the lodge, from which the former Sûreté man

waved to him with respectful familiarity. The Rolls was driving through the carriage entrance, with nobody behind the chauffeur. Maigret climbed to the first floor and rang the bell.

'Good afternoon, Ferdinand.'

Hadn't he become part of the household?

'I'll take you to madame.'

Ferdinand had been informed. She hadn't left anything to chance. Relieved of his hat, as if he was in a restaurant, he walked for the first time across a huge drawing room that wouldn't have looked out of place in a ministry. Not a single personal object left lying about, no scarf, no cigarette holder, no open book. No cigarette ends in the ashtrays. Three tall windows open on to the quiet courtyard, drenched now by the sun, where no cars were being washed.

A corridor. A bend. The apartment seemed to comprise a central body and two wings, like an old chateau. A strip of red carpet on the white marble tiled floor. Everywhere, those high ceilings that made you feel smaller.

Ferdinand knocked softly at a double door, opened it without waiting and announced:

'Detective Chief Inspector Maigret.'

He found himself in a boudoir. There was nobody there, but immediately Madame Parendon emerged from an adjoining room with her arm extended, walked up to Maigret and vigorously shook his hand.

'I feel embarrassed to have phoned you, inspector, or rather, to have phoned one of your employees.'

Here, everything was blue: the silk brocade covering

the walls, the Louis XV armchairs, the carpet; even the Chinese rug had a yellow pattern on a blue background.

Was it chance that she was still in a dressing gown, a turquoise blue dressing gown, at two in the afternoon?

'Forgive me for receiving you in this cubby hole, as I call it, but this is the only place where we won't be constantly disturbed.'

The door through which she had entered was still ajar, and he glimpsed a dressing table, also Louis XV, indicating that it was her bedroom.

'Please take a seat.'

She indicated a flimsy-looking armchair into which Maigret slid cautiously, vowing not to move too much.

'Do smoke your pipe.'

Even if he didn't feel like it! She wanted him to look just the way he did in newspaper photographs. The photographers never failed to remind him:

'Your pipe, inspector.'

As if he sucked at his pipe from morning to evening! What if he wanted to smoke a cigarette? A cigar? Or not smoke at all?

He didn't like the armchair he was sitting in – he expected to hear it crack at any moment. He didn't like this blue boudoir, this woman in blue giving him a veiled smile.

She had sat down in a wing chair and was lighting a cigarette with the help of a gold cigarette lighter, the kind he had seen in the window of Cartier's. The cigarette box was gold, too. A lot of things in these rooms were probably made of gold.

'I'm a little jealous that you've seen the Vague girl before me. This morning—'

'I wouldn't have dared disturb you so early.'

Was Maigret getting used to high society? He could have kicked himself for his own smooth demeanour.

'I assume you've been told that I get up late and dawdle in my bedroom until midday. It's both true and untrue. As it happens, I'm very active, Monsieur Maigret, and begin my days early. First of all, there's this large household to run. If I didn't call the suppliers myself, I don't know what we would eat, or what bills we'd get at the end of the month. Madame Vauquin's an excellent cook, but the telephone still terrifies her and makes her stammer. The children take up a lot of my time, too. Even though they're grown-up now, I still have to see about their clothes, their activities. If it weren't for me, Gus would live all year in drill trousers, a pullover and tennis sandals. Well, that's of no matter . . . There's also the charity work I do. Others merely send cheques or attend cocktail parties, but when there's real work to be done they all disappear . . .'

He was waiting, patiently, politely, so patiently and so politely that he couldn't get over it.

'I imagine you also lead a busy life.'

'You know, madame, I'm just a public servant, nothing more.'

She laughed, showing all her teeth and the tip of her pink tongue. He was struck by how pointed her tongue was. She was blonde, verging on ginger, with the kind of eyes that are called green but are most often a dull grey.

Was she forty? A little younger? A little older? Forty-five? The beauty salon had done its work so well, it was impossible to say.

'I'll have to tell that to Jacqueline. She's a good friend of mine, the wife of the minister of the interior.'

Well, now he knew! She hadn't wasted any time in playing her trump card.

'I may seem to be joking, and I do joke, but please believe me, it's only a façade. The fact is, Monsieur Maigret, I'm deeply disturbed by what's happening, although "disturbed" is too weak a word.'

Then, all at once:

'What do you think of my husband?'

'He's very pleasant.'

'Of course. That's what everyone says. What I mean is—'

'He's highly intelligent, remarkably intelligent in fact, and . . .'

She was becoming impatient. She knew where she wanted to get to, and he was cutting her off. Looking at her hands, Maigret observed that they were older than her face.

'I think he's also very sensitive.'

'If you were being completely honest, wouldn't you say over-sensitive?'

He opened his mouth, but this time she was the one who got in first.

'There are times he's so withdrawn, he scares me. He's a man who suffers a lot. I've always known that. When I married him, there was a certain amount of pity in my love.'

He feigned stupidity.

'Why?'

She was thrown for a moment.

'I mean . . . I mean, you saw him. Even when he was a child, he must have been ashamed of his physical appearance.'

'He isn't tall. But there are others who—'

'Come now, inspector,' she said irritably, 'let's be fair. I don't know what his family history has to do with it, or rather, I know only too well. His mother was a young nurse in Laennec, more precisely a ward orderly, and she was only sixteen when Professor Parendon got her pregnant. Why, being a surgeon, didn't he operate on her? Did she threaten to cause a scandal? I don't know. What I do know is that Émile was born premature, at seven months.'

'Most premature babies grow up normal children.'

'Do you think he's normal?'

'In what sense?'

She nervously extinguished her cigarette and lit another.

'Forgive me. I have the impression that you're dodging the issue, that you don't want to understand.'

'Understand what?'

Unable to hold out any longer, she sprang to her feet and started pacing up and down the Chinese rug.

'Understand why I'm worried sick! For more than twenty years, I've worked hard to protect him, to make him happy, to give him a normal life.'

He sat watching her and smoking his pipe in silence. She was wearing very elegant slippers that must have been made to measure.

'Those letters he told me about. I've no idea who wrote them, but they fit in well with my anxiety.'

'How long have you been anxious?'

'Weeks . . . Months . . . I don't dare say years . . . When we were first married, he did whatever I did, we went out together, went to the theatre, had dinner out.'

'Did it cheer him up?'

'At least it relaxed him. But now I suspect that he doesn't feel at home anywhere, that he's ashamed of not being like everybody else and always has been . . . Look, even the choice of maritime law as a career. Can you tell me why a man like him would choose maritime law? It was an act of defiance. Not being able to plead in court—'

'Why not?'

She gave him a disappointed look.

'Come, now, Monsieur Maigret, you know as well as I do. Can you see that pale, insubstantial little man pleading for a man's life in a courtroom?'

He preferred not to retort that there had been an important lawyer in the last century who was only one metre fifty-five tall.

'He mopes about. As time passes and he gets older, he locks himself in more and more, and, when we give a dinner party, it's the devil's own job to get him to take part.'

Nor did he ask her:

'Who draws up the guest list?'

He was watching and listening. He was watching and trying not to let it bother him, because the picture that this woman with her fraught nerves and fiery energy was painting of her husband was both true and false.

But what was true and what was false?

That was what he would have liked to untangle. The image of Émile Parendon was starting to seem like a blurred photograph. The outlines lacked clarity, and the features kept changing expression depending on the angle from which you looked at them.

It was true that he had shut himself up in a world of his own – in the world of Article 64, perhaps. Was man responsible for his actions or not? He wasn't the only one fascinated by this crucial question. In the Middle Ages, there had been councils to discuss it.

Had this idea become an obsession for Parendon? Maigret remembered walking into the office the day before and the look that Parendon had given him, as if at that moment Maigret represented a kind of embodiment of the famous article or was capable of providing an answer.

Parendon hadn't asked him what he had come for, what he wanted. He had talked to him about Article 64, his lips almost quivering with emotion.

It was true that . . .

Yes, he led an almost solitary existence in this apartment that was too large for him, like a giant's jacket.

How, with his puny body, with all the thoughts running round and round in his head, could he deal every day with a woman so full of nervous energy that she transmitted that energy to everything around her?

It was true that he was a runt! Yes, even a gnome.

But every now and again, when the adjoining rooms seemed empty, when the opportunity presented itself, he and Mademoiselle Vague made love.

What was true? What was false? Wasn't Bambi protecting herself from her mother by taking refuge in archaeology?

'Listen to me, Monsieur Maigret. I'm not the frivolous woman others may have described to you. I'm a woman with responsibilities, a woman who tries her best to make herself useful. That's how our father raised my sisters and me. He was a man who believed in duty.'

Oh, dear! Maigret wasn't at all keen on these words: the upright magistrate, a credit to the profession, teaching his daughters the meaning of duty . . .

And yet, coming from her, it didn't sound all that false. She didn't give her mind time to linger on any one sentence because her face kept moving, her whole body kept moving, and one word followed another, one idea followed another, one image followed another, in rapid succession.

'There is fear in this house, it's true. And I'm the one who feels it most. Oh, don't go thinking I wrote you those letters! I'm too direct to go about things in such a roundabout way. If I'd wanted to see you, I'd have telephoned as I did this morning . . . I'm afraid. Not so much for myself as for him. What he can do, I don't know, but I sense that he'll do something, that he's at the end of his tether, that some kind of demon inside him is urging him to do something dramatic.'

'What makes you think that?'

'You've seen him, haven't you?'

'He struck me as very calm and level-headed, and I even thought he had quite a sophisticated sense of humour.'

'Oh, he has a sense of humour, but it's dark, even macabre. The man is sick with worry. His business takes up no more than two or three days a week. René Tortu does most of his research for him. He reads reviews and sends letters all over the world to people he doesn't know whose articles he's read. He sometimes doesn't set foot outside for days on end, just watches the world through the window. The same chestnut trees, the same wall around the garden of the Élysée, I was going to add the same people passing in the street . . . You came twice and didn't ask to see me. But unfortunately, I'm the one who's most involved. I'm his wife, don't forget that, even though he sometimes seems to forget it. We have two children who still need guidance.'

She paused for breath and lit a cigarette. It was the fourth one. She smoked greedily, while still talking just as fast, and the boudoir was already filled with clouds of smoke.

'I don't think you can predict what he'll do, any more than I can. Is it himself he'll harm? It's possible, and I'd be terribly upset, having tried for so many years to make him happy. Is it my fault I haven't succeeded? Or perhaps I'll be the victim, yes, that's more likely, because he's gradually started to hate me. Can you understand that? His brother, who's a neurologist, might be able to explain it. He needs to project his disappointment, his resentment, his humiliation on to someone.'

'Forgive me if—'

'Please let me finish. Tomorrow, the day after tomorrow, or whenever, you may be called here to look at a corpse, and that corpse will be me. I forgive him in advance, because I know he isn't responsible and that in spite of the progress that medicine has made—'

'Do you consider your husband a medical case?'

She looked at him with a kind of defiance.

'Yes.'

'A mental case?'

'Perhaps.'

'Have you spoken to doctors?'

'Yes.'

'Doctors who know him?'

'We have several doctors among our friends.'

'What exactly did they tell you?'

'To be careful.'

'Careful about what?'

'We didn't go into details. These weren't consultations, but conversations during social occasions.'

'Did they all say the same thing?'

'Several of them, yes.'

'Can you give me any names?'

Maigret deliberately took his black notebook from his pocket. That was enough for her to beat a retreat.

'It wouldn't be right for me to give you their names, but if you want to have him examined by an expert . . .'

Maigret had lost his patient, good-humoured air. His features were tense, too, because things were starting to go too far.

'When you called my office to ask me to come and see you, did you already have that idea in your mind?'

'What idea?'

'To ask me more or less directly to have your husband examined by a psychiatrist.'

'Did I say that? I didn't even use that word.'

'But it's implied in everything you've said.'

'If that's the case, you've misunderstood me, or else I haven't expressed myself well. Perhaps I'm too frank, too spontaneous. I don't choose my words carefully. What I said, and I repeat it now, is that I'm afraid, that there's a sense of fear in this household.'

'And I repeat: fear of what?'

She sat down, as if exhausted, and looked at him with disappointment.

'I don't know what else to tell you, inspector. I thought you would understand without my needing to make it too clear. I'm afraid for him, for me.'

'In other words, afraid he'll kill you or commit suicide?'

'Put like that, it seems ridiculous, I know, when everything seems so peaceful here.'

'Forgive me for asking a personal question. Do you and your husband still have sexual relations?'

'Up until a year ago.'

'What happened a year ago to change things?'

'I caught him with that girl.'

'Mademoiselle Vague?'

'Yes.'

'In the office?'

'It was horrible.'

'And since then you've shut your door to him? Has he ever tried to get through?'

'Only once. I gave him a piece of my mind, and he understood.'

'He didn't insist?'

'He didn't even apologize. He slunk away like someone who's stepped out on the wrong floor.'

'Have you had lovers?'

'What?'

Her eyes had grown hard, her gaze sharp and malicious.

'I asked you,' he repeated calmly, 'if you've had lovers. These things happen, don't they?'

'Not in our family, inspector, and if my father were here—'

'As a magistrate, your father would understand that it's my duty to ask you the question. You've just told me about a general fear, a threat hanging over you or your husband. You imply that I should have him examined by a psychiatrist. Therefore it's only natural that—'

'I'm sorry. I got carried away. No, I haven't had lovers, and I never will have.'

'Do you own a gun?'

She stood up, walked briskly to the next room, came back and handed Maigret a little mother-of-pearl revolver.

'Careful. It's loaded.'

'Have you had it a long time?'

'A friend who really did have a dark sense of humour gave it to me when I got married.'

'Aren't you afraid that the children, as a game—'

'They don't often come into my room, and when they were younger this weapon used to be in a locked drawer.'

'What about your rifles?'

'They're in a case, and the case is in the shed, with our trunks, our suitcases and our golf bags.'

'Does your husband play golf?'

'I've tried to get him interested, but by the time he gets to the third hole, he's out of breath.'

'Is he often ill?'

'He hasn't had many serious illnesses. The worst, if I remember, was pleurisy. On the other hand, he's constantly getting sore throats, bouts of laryngitis and flu, head colds.'

'Does he call his doctor?'

'Of course.'

'Is he a friend of yours?'

'No. He's a local doctor, Dr Martin, who lives in Rue du Cirque, just behind here.'

'Has Dr Martin ever taken you aside?'

'No, he hasn't, but I've sometimes waited for him when he came out to ask him if there's anything seriously wrong with my husband.'

'What did he say?'

'He said no. He said it's men like him who live the longest. He mentioned Voltaire, who—'

'I know all about Voltaire . . . Did he ever suggest your husband consult a specialist?'

'No. Only . . .'

'Only . . . ?'

'What's the point? You're going to misinterpret my words again.'

'Try anyway.'

'I sense from your attitude that my husband made a

very good impression on you, as I was sure he would. I won't say that he's knowingly playing a role. With strangers, he's cheerful and appears very well-balanced. With Dr Martin, he talks and behaves as he does with you.'

'And with the staff?'

'He's not responsible for the work of the servants.'

'Meaning what?'

'That it's not up to him to reprimand them. He leaves that to me, with the result that I look like the bad one.'

Maigret was stifling in his overly snug armchair, in this boudoir where all the blue was starting to be unbearable to him. Getting to his feet, he almost stretched as he would have done in his office.

'Do you have anything more to tell me?'

Also now standing up, she looked him up and down as if they were equals.

'There would be no point.'

'Would you like me to send an inspector to keep guard in the apartment?'

'That's a perfectly absurd idea.'

'Not if I'm to believe your premonitions.'

'They aren't premonitions.'

'They aren't facts either.'

'Not yet.'

'Let's sum up. For some time now, your husband has been giving signs of mental disorder.'

'You will insist, won't you?'

'He's become increasingly withdrawn and his behaviour worries you.'

'That's closer to the truth.'

'You fear for his life or for yours.'

'Yes, I admit that.'

'Which do you think is more likely?'

'If I knew that, it would be some kind of relief.'

'Someone who lives in this apartment or has ready access to it has sent us two letters announcing an imminent crime. I should tell you that there was also a telephone call in my absence.'

'Why didn't you tell me that before?'

'Because I was listening to you . . . This call, which was very brief, simply confirmed what was in the letters. What the caller said was basically: "Tell Inspector Maigret it'll happen soon."'

He saw her turn pale. She wasn't play-acting. Her face suddenly became colourless, apart from a few patches of make-up, and the corners of her lips drooped.

'Oh!'

She lowered her head, and her thin body seemed to have lost its prodigious energy.

At that moment, he forgot his irritation and felt sorry for her.

'Are you sure you don't want me to send someone?'

'What's the point?'

'What do you mean?'

'If something is meant to happen, a policeman being somewhere in the apartment won't prevent it.'

'Did you know that your husband owns an automatic?'

'Yes.'

'And does he know that you own this revolver?'

'Of course.'

'What about your children?'

Ready to weep with annoyance, she cried:

'My children have nothing to do with all this, don't you understand? They don't care about us, only themselves. They have their own lives to get on with. They don't give a damn about ours, what's left of it.'

She had again spoken vehemently, as if certain subjects automatically set her off.

'Well, there you are! Forgive me if I don't see you out . . . I wonder what it was I expected . . . What will be, will be! Go and see my husband again, or that girl . . . Goodbye, Monsieur Maigret.'

She had opened the door for him and waited for him to leave before shutting it. Once out in the corridor, it already seemed to Maigret that he was emerging from another world. All that blue he had just left still haunted him.

Through a window, he looked out at the courtyard, where a different chauffeur from the one in the morning was polishing a different car. It was still sunny, and there was a light breeze.

He was tempted to get his hat from the cloakroom, with which he was familiar, and to leave without saying anything. Then, almost reluctantly, he walked to Mademoiselle Vague's office.

A white coat over her dress, she was photocopying documents. The blinds were closed, letting only thin rays of light filter in.

'Were you hoping to see Monsieur Parendon?'

'No.'

'Just as well. He's in a meeting with two important

clients, one from Amsterdam, the other from Athens. They're both shipowners, and they . . .'

He wasn't listening. She went and opened the blinds, and the sun streamed in.

'You look tired.'

'I just spent an hour with Madame Parendon.'

'I know.'

He looked at the switchboard.

'Was it you who put her through to Quai des Orfèvres?'

'No. I didn't even know she'd phoned. I heard it from Lise when she came to ask me for a stamp.'

'Tell me about Lise.'

'She's the maid.'

'I know that. I'm asking what kind of person she is.'

'A simple girl like me. We're both from the provinces. I'm from a small town, and she's from the country. As I had a bit of education, I became a secretary, and as she didn't have any, she became a maid.'

'How old is she?'

'Twenty-three. I know everyone's age, because I fill out the Social Security forms.'

'Is she conscientious?'

'Whatever she's told to do, she does well. I don't think she has any desire to change jobs.'

'Any boyfriends?'

'Yes, on her day off, which is Saturday.'

'Is she bright enough to write the letters you read?'

'Definitely not.'

'Did you know that Madame Parendon caught you with her husband about a year ago?'

'I told you it happened once, but there may have been other times when she opened and closed the door without making any noise.'

'Did Parendon tell you that, ever since, his wife has been refusing to have sex with him?'

'They didn't have it that often anyway!'

'Why not?'

'Because he doesn't love her.'

'Doesn't love her or doesn't love her any more?'

'That depends on what you mean by the word "love". I suppose he was grateful to her for marrying him and for years tried his best to show his gratitude.'

Maigret smiled at the thought that, on the other side of the wall, two important oil magnates from opposite ends of Europe were putting their wealth in the hands of the little man he and Mademoiselle Vague were talking about in this way.

For them he wasn't a colourless, half-helpless gnome, withdrawn and brooding on unhealthy thoughts, but one of the leading lights of maritime law. Weren't the three of them playing with hundreds of millions while Madame Parendon, angry or demoralized, disappointed in any case, was getting ready for her four o'clock appointment?

'Wouldn't you like to sit down?'

'I think I'll have a look next door.'

'You'll only find Julien Baud there. Tortu's at the Palais de Justice.'

He made a vague gesture.

'Julien Baud will do!'

4.

Maigret might have thought he was entering a different apartment. In contrast to the orderliness of the rest of the place, frozen as it was in the solemn atmosphere established by Chief Justice Gassin de Beaulieu, what was immediately striking about the office that René Tortu shared with young Julien Baud was the untidiness, the air of sloppiness.

By the window stood a desk, the kind found in all commercial offices, cluttered with files, and there were green binders on pine shelves, piled one on top of the other as the need arose. There were even some on the polished wooden floor.

As for Julien Baud's desk, it was a former kitchen table covered in wrapping paper held on with drawing pins. On the wall, stuck on with adhesive tape, were pictures of naked women cut out of magazines. As Maigret opened the door, Baud was busy weighing and stamping envelopes. He raised his head and looked at him without surprise or alarm, as if wondering what he was doing here.

'Are you looking for Tortu?'

'No. I know he's at the Palais de Justice.'

'He'll be back soon.'

'It's not him I'm looking for.'

'Who, then?'

'Nobody.'

A well-built, red-haired young man with freckles on his cheeks. His porcelain-blue eyes expressed total calm.

'Would you like to sit down?'

'No.'

'Suit yourself.'

He continued weighing letters, some of them in large-format manila envelopes, then consulting a little book that indicated the postage rates for different countries.

'Having fun?' Maigret asked.

'Oh, you know, as long as I'm in Paris . . .'

He had a delightful hint of an accent and dragged out some of the syllables.

'Where are you from?'

'Morges, on the shores of Lake Léman. Do you know it?'

'I've been through there.'

'Pretty, isn't it?'

'Yes, it is . . . What's it like to work here?'

'It's a big place,' Baud replied, slightly misunderstanding the question.

'How do you get on with Monsieur Parendon?'

'I don't see much of him. I put stamps on envelopes, I go to the post office, I run errands, I wrap parcels. I'm not exactly important. Every now and again, the boss comes in, pats me on the shoulder and asks: "Everything all right, young man?" The servants all call me "the little Swiss", even though I'm one metre eighty tall.'

'Do you get on well with Mademoiselle Vague?'

'She's nice to me.'

'What do you think of her?'

'Well, you know, she's also on the other side of the wall, the boss's side.'

'What do you mean?'

'I mean, they have their work there, and we have ours here. When the boss needs someone, he doesn't call for me, he calls for her.'

There was an innocent expression on his face, but Maigret wasn't sure this innocence wasn't feigned.

'I hear you want to be a playwright?'

'I try to write plays. I've written two so far, but they're no good. When you come from the canton of Vaud like me, you have to get used to Paris first.'

'Does Tortu help you?'

'Help me with what?'

'Getting to know Paris. By taking you out, for instance.'

'He's never taken me out. He has other things to do.'

'Like what?'

'See his fiancée, his friends . . . As soon as I got off the train at Gare de Lyon, I realized it's every man for himself here.'

'Do you often see Madame Parendon?'

'Quite often, especially in the mornings. When she's forgotten to phone a supplier, she comes to see me. "Dear boy, would you be so kind as to order a leg of lamb and ask for it to be delivered right away? If they don't have anyone, pop over to the butcher's yourself, would you?" So I go to the butcher's, the fishmonger's, the grocer's. I go to her bootmaker's if there's a scratch on her shoe. It's always "dear boy". It's either that or putting stamps on envelopes.'

'What do you think of her?'

'I may put her in one of my plays.'

'Because she's such an extraordinary character?'

'Nobody here is ordinary. They're all crazy.'

'Your boss, too?'

'He's intelligent, of course, or he wouldn't be in the profession he's in, but he's a fanatic, right? With all the money he makes, he could at least do something more than just sit behind his desk or in an armchair. OK, he may not be very strong, but all the same . . .'

'Are you aware of his relationship with Mademoiselle Vague?'

'Everyone is. But he could afford dozens of girls, hundreds of them, if you see what I mean.'

'What about his relations with his wife?'

'What relations? They live in the same apartment, they meet in the corridors the way people pass each other in the street. Once, I had to go into the dining room during lunch, because I was alone in the office and I'd just received an urgent telegram. Well, they were sitting there like strangers in a restaurant.'

'You don't seem to be especially fond of them.'

'I could have done worse. At least they provide me with characters.'

'Comic ones?'

'Comic and tragic at the same time. Just like life.'

'Have you heard about the letters?'

'Of course.'

'Do you have any idea who wrote them?'

'It could be anybody. It could be me.'

'And is it?'

'No. It never occurred to me.'

'Does the daughter get on well with you?'

'Mademoiselle Bambi?' He shrugged. 'I wonder if she'd even recognize me in the street. When she needs something – paper, scissors, whatever – she comes in, doesn't say a word, just helps herself and goes out again.'

'Is she arrogant?'

'Maybe not . . . Maybe it's just her nature.'

'Do you also think something terrible might happen?'

He looked at Maigret with his big blue eyes.

'Something terrible can happen anywhere. Last year, for instance, on a day as sunny as today, a sweet little old lady out for a walk was knocked down by a bus just outside the building. A few seconds earlier, she'd had no idea—'

They heard hurried steps in the corridor. A brown-haired young man of about thirty, of medium height, stopped dead in the doorway.

'Come in, Monsieur Tortu.'

He was carrying a briefcase and had a self-important air.

'Inspector Maigret, I assume?'

'You assume correctly.'

'Is it me you want to see? Have you been waiting long?'

'Actually, I'm not waiting for anyone.'

He was quite a handsome young man, with dark hair, well-drawn features and an aggressive expression. He was clearly someone determined to make his way in life.

'Won't you sit down?' he asked, walking over to the desk and putting his briefcase down on it.

'I've been sitting for a good part of the day. Your young colleague and I were chatting.'

The word 'colleague' clearly shocked René Tortu, who glared at Baud.

'I had an important case to deal with at the Palais de Justice.'

'I know. Do you often appear in court?'

'Whenever mediation proves impossible. Maître Parendon seldom appears in person. We prepare the files together and then I get to plead the case.'

'I see.'

Tortu clearly had no doubts about his own importance.

'What do you think of Maître Parendon?'

'As a man or as a jurist?'

'Both.'

'As a jurist, he's far beyond his peers, and nobody has his skill at spotting the weak point in the opponent's argument.'

'And as a man?'

'Working for him, being his only close colleague, so to speak, it's not up to me to judge him in that respect.'

'Do you think he's weak?'

'That's not the word I would have used. Let's just say that if I were him, and at his age, I'd lead a more active life.'

'Being present at the parties his wife gives, for instance, going to the theatre with her, dining out?'

'Perhaps. You can't live surrounded by nothing but books and files.'

'Have you read the letters?'

'Maître Parendon showed me the photostats.'

'Do you think they're a hoax?'

'Perhaps. I must admit I haven't given it much thought.'

'Even though they suggest that something bad is going to happen here soon?'

Tortu said nothing. He took papers from his briefcase and put them away in the binders.

'Would you marry a girl who was a younger version of Madame Parendon?'

Tortu looked at him in surprise.

'I'm already engaged, or haven't you heard? So there's no question of—'

'It was my way of asking you what you think of her.'

'She's active, intelligent, and is able to get on well with—'

He turned abruptly towards the door, and there in the doorway stood the woman they were talking about. She was wearing a leopard-skin coat over a black silk dress. Either she was about to go out, or she had just got back.

'You're still here,' she said in surprise, turning her calm, cold gaze on Maigret.

'As you can see.'

It was difficult to know how long she had been standing in the corridor or how much of the conversation she had heard. Maigret understood what Mademoiselle Vague had meant when she had talked about a household where you never knew if you were being spied on.

'Dear boy,' she said to Baud, 'could you call the Countess of Prange immediately and let her know I'll be at least a quarter of an hour late because I was detained at the last moment? Mademoiselle Vague is busy with my husband and these gentlemen.'

She gave Maigret a final harsh look and left the room. Julien Baud picked up the telephone. As for Tortu, he was presumably pleased: if Madame Parendon had heard his last answers, she couldn't help but be grateful to him.

'Hello? Is that the Countess of Prange's residence?'

Maigret shrugged slightly and left the room. Julien Baud amused him, and he had a feeling the boy would do well as a playwright. As for Tortu, he didn't like him, but for no particular reason.

Mademoiselle Vague's door was open, but the office was empty. Passing Parendon's office, he heard a murmur of voices.

Just as he reached the cloakroom to get his hat, Ferdinand appeared as if by chance.

'Do you stand by the door all day?'

'No, inspector. I just thought you'd be leaving soon. Madame went out a few minutes ago.'

'I know. Have you ever been in prison, Ferdinand?'

'Just military prison, in Africa.'

'Are you French?'

'Yes, from Aubagne.'

'How did you come to join the Foreign Legion?'

'I was young. I'd done a few stupid things.'

'In Aubagne?'

'In Toulon. You know how it is, I'd got into bad company. When I realized things were about to go wrong, I joined the Legion. I told them I was Belgian.'

'And you've never been in trouble since?'

'I've been in Monsieur Parendon's service for eight years, and he's never had any complaints about me.'

'Do you like the job?'

'There are worse ones.'

'Is Monsieur Parendon good to you?'

'He's the best of men.'

'What about madame?'

'Between you and me, she's a bitch.'

'Does she give you a hard time?'

'She gives everyone a hard time. She's everywhere, checks on everything, complains about everything. It's a good thing I have my room over the garage.'

'To have your girlfriends round?'

'If I made the mistake of doing that and she found out, she'd fire me on the spot. As far as she's concerned, servants ought to be neutered. But at least being over there means I can breathe in peace. I can also go out when I feel like it, although I'm linked to the apartment by a bell and I'm supposed to be on call, as she puts it, twenty-four hours a day.'

'Has she ever sent for you at night?'

'Three or four times. To make sure I was there, I suppose.'

'On what pretext?'

'Once, she'd heard a suspicious noise and she went round all the rooms with me looking for a burglar.'

'What was it, a cat?'

'There are no cats or dogs in the apartment. She wouldn't allow them. When Monsieur Gus was younger, he asked for a puppy for Christmas but instead got an electric train set. I've never seen a boy throw a tantrum like that.'

'What about the other times?'

'One other time, it was a smell of burning. The third time . . . Hold on. Oh, yes! She'd listened at monsieur's door and hadn't heard him breathing. She sent me to see if he was all right.'

'Couldn't she have gone herself?'

'I suppose she had her reasons. I'm not complaining, mind you. Since she goes out every afternoon and most evenings, there are long periods when it's quiet.'

'Do you get on well with Lise?'

'Quite well. She's a pretty girl. For a while . . . Well, you know what I mean . . . But she likes change . . . A different man almost every Saturday . . . And since I don't like to share . . .'

'What about Madame Vauquin?'

'She's an old cow!'

'Doesn't she like you?'

'She measures out our portions like we were school-kids, and she's even stricter with the wine, I guess because her husband's a drunkard who beats her at least twice a week . . . Because of that, she hates all men.'

'And Madame Marchand?'

'Almost the only time I see her is when she's vacuuming. She's the kind of woman who never opens her mouth, just moves her lips when she's alone. Maybe she's praying.'

'What about mademoiselle?'

'She isn't proud or fussy. A pity she's always so sad.'

'Do you think she's unhappy in love?'

'I don't know. Maybe it's just the atmosphere of this place.'

'Have you heard about the letters?'

He appeared embarrassed.

'I might as well tell you the truth. Yes. But I haven't read them.'

'Who told you about them?'

Even more embarrassed, he pretended to search in his memory.

'I don't know. The thing is, I come and go, I say a few words to this person or that . . .'

'Was it Mademoiselle Vague?'

'No, she never talks about monsieur's business.'

'Monsieur Tortu?'

'He looks at me like he was a second boss.'

'Julien Baud?'

'Maybe. To be honest, I don't remember. Maybe it was in the servants' room.'

'Do you know if there are any guns in the apartment?'

'Monsieur has a .38 in the drawer of his bedside table, but I haven't seen cartridges in the room.'

'Do you clean his room?'

'It's part of my job. I also serve at table, of course.'

'Do you know of any other guns?'

'Madame's little toy, a 6.33 manufactured in Herstal. You'd have to fire that from very close up to hurt anyone.'

'Have you sensed any change in the atmosphere here lately?'

He seemed to be searching his memory.

'It's possible. They never talk much when they sit down to meals. These days, I guess they don't talk at all. Sometimes just a few sentences between Monsieur Gus and mademoiselle.'

'Do you believe the letters?'

'The way I believe in astrology. According to the horoscopes in the newspaper, I should receive a large sum of money at least once a week.'

'So you don't think something might happen?'

'Not because of the letters.'

'Because of what?'

'I don't know.'

'Does Monsieur Parendon seem strange to you?'

'Depends what you call strange. Everyone has their own idea about the life they lead. If he's happy like that . . . Anyway, he's not crazy. In fact, probably the opposite.'

'Do you think she's the one who's crazy?'

'Not that either! Oh, no! The woman's as crafty as a fox.'

'Many thanks, Ferdinand.'

'I did my best, inspector. I've learned that it's always best to be honest with the police.'

The door closed behind Maigret, who walked down the big staircase with its wrought-iron banister. He waved at the concierge, who looked in his livery like the doorman of a luxury hotel, and sighed with pleasure when he found himself back out in the cool air.

He remembered a pleasant bar on the corner of Avenue Marigny and Rue du Cirque. He went in and headed straight for the counter. He thought about what to drink and finally ordered a draught beer. The atmosphere of the

Parendons' apartment still clung to his body. But wouldn't it have been the same if he had spent so much time with any family?

Less intense, perhaps, although he would probably have found the same resentments, the same petty-minded thoughts, the same fears, certainly the same inconsistencies.

'Stop philosophizing, Maigret!'

Wasn't it a principle of his to forbid himself from thinking? All right, then! He hadn't seen the two children, or the cook, or the cleaner. He had only caught a glimpse of the maid in her black uniform, with her little embroidered apron and cap.

Being on the corner of Rue du Cirque, he remembered Dr Martin, Parendon's personal doctor.

'How much do I owe you?'

He saw the doctor's nameplate outside the building, climbed to the third floor and was admitted to a waiting room. There were already three people there. Discouraged, he made to leave.

'Aren't you going to wait for the doctor?'

'I didn't come for a consultation. I'll phone him.'

'What name shall I say?'

'Detective Chief Inspector Maigret.'

'Don't you want me to tell him you're here?'

'I'd rather not keep his patients waiting any longer.'

There was the other Parendon, the brother, but he was a doctor, too, and thanks to his friend Pardon, Maigret had a good idea what the lives of doctors in Paris were like.

He didn't feel like taking the bus or the Métro. He felt weary, swollen with fatigue, and he collapsed into the back seat of a taxi.

'Quai des Orfèvres.'

'Yes, Monsieur Maigret.'

It no longer gave him any pleasure. He had once been quite proud of being recognized like this, but for some years now it had been more irritating than anything else.

How would he look if nothing happened in the apartment on Avenue Marigny? He hadn't even dared mention the letters at the daily briefing. For two days, he had been neglecting his office, spending most of his time in an apartment where people led a life that was no concern of his.

There were cases in progress, not very major ones, fortunately, but ones he should at least deal with.

Had the letters, plus the telephone call at midday, distorted his view of these people? He couldn't think of Madame Parendon as just any woman you might meet in the street. He saw her again, pathetic in all the blue of her boudoir and her dressing gown, performing a kind of tragedy for his benefit.

Parendon, too, had stopped being a man like any other. The gnome would look at him with those clear eyes of his, enlarged by the thick lenses of his glasses, and Maigret would try in vain to read his thoughts in them.

The others . . . Mademoiselle Vague . . . That big redhead Julien Baud . . . Tortu suddenly turning to look at the door where Madame Parendon had appeared as if by a miracle . . .

He shrugged and, as the taxi drew up outside the gate of the Police Judiciaire, he searched in his pockets for change.

A dozen inspectors paraded through his office, each with a problem to submit to him. He went through the mail that had arrived in his absence and signed a pile of documents, but in all the time he worked like this, in the gilded calm of his office, the apartment on Avenue Marigny was still somewhere in the background.

He felt an unease he couldn't dispel. And yet up until now he had done all he could. No crime had been committed. Nobody had called the police officially to report a specific act. Nobody had lodged a complaint.

He had nevertheless devoted hours to studying the small group of people that gravitated around Émile Parendon.

He looked in his memory for a precedent but couldn't find one, even though he had known the most diverse situations.

At 5.15, he was brought an express letter that had just arrived and immediately recognized the block capitals.

The seal indicated that the letter had been sent from the post office in Rue de Miromesnil at 4.30. In other words, fifteen minutes after he'd left the Parendons'.

He cut the band along the dotted line. Because of the size of the paper, the characters were smaller than in the previous letters. It was clear to Maigret, when he compared them, that this one had been written more quickly and with less care, perhaps in a state of heightened excitement.

Detective chief inspector,

When I wrote you my first letter and asked you to reply by means of a small ad, I never imagined that you would plunge straight into this case, as I had been planning to subsequently provide you with the details you needed.

Your haste has spoiled everything, and now you must realize yourself that you are floundering. Today, you provoked the murderer in a way, and I am convinced that because of you they will feel obliged to strike.

I may be wrong, but I think it will be in the next few hours. I can no longer help you. I am sorry. I bear you no ill will.

Gravely, Maigret read and reread this note, then walked over to the door and called Janvier and Lapointe. Lucas was absent.

'Read this, boys.'

He observed them with a certain anxiety, as if wanting to see if they would react in the same way as he had. Unlike him, they hadn't been befuddled by hours spent in the apartment. They were able to judge for themselves.

Looking at the letter together, they both showed a growing interest, which turned to concern.

'Things seemed to be getting clearer,' Janvier said, putting the letter down on the desk.

'What are these people like?' Lapointe asked.

'Like everyone and no one. The thing I'm wondering is what we can do. I can't leave a man on duty in the apartment, and there'd be no point anyway. The place is so vast, anything can happen at one end without anyone noticing at the other end. Have someone guard the building? I'm going to do that tonight, to be on the safe side, but if these messages aren't a hoax, the blow won't come from outside . . . Are you free, Lapointe?'

'I have nothing special to do, chief.'

'I'd like you to go over there. The concierge is a man named Lamure, who used to be in the Sûreté. I want you to spend the night in his lodge, going up to the first floor every now and again. Get Lamure to give you a list of everyone living in the building, including staff, and make a note of who goes in and out.'

'I get the idea.'

'What idea?'

'That in this way, if something happens, we'll at least have a basis.'

It was true, but Maigret hated envisaging the situation in that light. If something happens . . . They weren't talking about a burglary, but about murder. But who would be murdered? And by whom?

A number of people had talked to him, answered his questions, apparently confessed certain things. Damn it, was it for him to judge who was lying and who was telling the truth, let alone whether one of those involved was mad?

He paced his office with big, almost angry strides, speaking as if to himself, while Lapointe and Janvier exchanged glances.

'It's quite simple, inspector. Someone writes to tell you there's going to be a murder. Only, they can't tell you in advance who's going to kill whom, or when, or how. Why contact you? Why warn you? For no reason. To play a game.'

He grabbed a pipe and filled it with nervous jabs of his index finger.

'I mean, what do they take me for? If something happens, they'll claim it's my fault. This latest letter is already claiming as much. Apparently, I was too hasty. But what else was I supposed to do? Wait to receive an announcement? And if nothing happens, I'll look like an idiot, I'll be the man who wasted taxpayers' money for two whole days.'

Janvier kept a straight face, but Lapointe couldn't help smiling, and Maigret noticed. His anger hung in the air for a moment. At last, he, too, smiled and patted the young man on the shoulder.

'I'm sorry, boys. This business is getting to me. Everyone there tiptoes around, and I've started doing the same, as if I'm walking on eggshells.'

This time, at the image of Maigret walking on eggshells, Janvier was forced to laugh, too.

'Here, at least, I can give vent. It's over now. Let's get down to business. Lapointe, go and have something to eat, then get over to Avenue Marigny. If anything suspicious happens, don't hesitate to call me at home, even if it's the middle of the night. Good night. I'll see you tomorrow. Someone will relieve you at eight in the morning.'

He went to the window and stood there looking down at the line of the Seine.

'What are you working on right now?' he asked Janvier.

'I arrested the two boys this morning, two sixteen-year-olds. You were right . . .'

'Would you mind taking over from Lapointe tomorrow? It seems stupid, I know, and of course that's why I'm so angry, but I feel I have to take these precautions even if there's no point to them. If something happens, everyone will lash out at me, you'll see.'

As he uttered these last words, his eyes came to rest on one of the lamp posts on Pont Saint-Michel.

'Pass me the letter.'

He'd remembered a word from the letter. He hadn't paid any attention to it earlier, and he wondered if his memory was playing tricks with him.

> . . . I am convinced that because of you they will feel obliged to strike . . .

Yes, the word *strike* was definitely there. Obviously, it could mean simply take action. But in all three letters, the anonymous writer had been quite meticulous in his choice of words.

' "Strike", do you get it? The husband and the wife both have guns. I was actually thinking of asking them to hand them over to us, the way you take matches away from children. But I can't take away all the kitchen knives, all the paper knives. You can strike with andirons too, and as there's no lack of fireplaces . . . Or with candlesticks. Or statuettes . . .'

Suddenly changing tone, he said:

'Try and get me Germain Parendon on the phone. He's a neurologist who lives in Rue d'Aguesseau, the brother of my Parendon.'

While Janvier, sitting on a corner of the desk, dealt with the telephone, Maigret took the opportunity to relight his pipe.

'Hello? Have I reached Dr Parendon? . . . Police Judiciaire, mademoiselle. The office of Detective Chief Inspector Maigret. Monsieur Maigret would like a few words with the doctor . . . What? In Nice? . . . Yes . . . Just a moment.'

Maigret had been signalling to him.

'Ask her where he's staying.'

'Are you still there? Could you tell me where the doctor is staying? . . . The Negresco? . . . Thank you . . . Yes, I suspect he is. I'll try anyway.'

'Is he seeing a patient?'

'No, he's at a conference on child neurology. Apparently they have a full schedule, and the doctor is due to present a paper tomorrow.'

'Call the Negresco. It's six o'clock. The session must be over by now. At eight, they're probably all going to dinner somewhere, at the Préfecture or wherever. If he isn't already at some cocktail party or other.'

They had to wait about ten minutes, the Negresco being constantly engaged.

'Hello? This is the Police Judiciaire in Paris, mademoiselle. Could you please put me through to Dr Parendon? . . . Parendon, yes. He's one of the conference delegates.'

Janvier put his hand over the receiver.

'She's going to see if he's in his room or at the cocktail party that's taking place right now in the big room on the mezzanine . . . Hello? . . . Yes, doctor . . . I'm sorry about that. Let me pass you Detective Chief Inspector Maigret.'

Maigret felt awkward as he took the receiver, unsure at the last moment as to what to say.

'I'm sorry to disturb you, doctor.'

'I was just about to go over my paper one last time.'

'As I assumed. Yesterday and today, I spent quite a long time with your brother.'

'How did you happen to meet my brother?'

The voice was cheerful and friendly, and much younger than Maigret had imagined.

'It's rather a complicated story, and that's why I've taken the liberty of calling you.'

'Is my brother in any trouble?'

'If he is, it's not the kind that concerns us.'

'Is he ill?'

'What do you think of his health?'

'He seems a lot frailer and weaker than he really is. I'd be quite incapable of all the work he manages to get through in a few days.'

It was necessary to go all the way.

'I'm going to explain the situation as briefly as possible. Yesterday morning, I received an anonymous letter saying that a murder was probably going to be committed.'

'At Émile's?'

There was laughter in the voice.

'No. It would take too long to tell you how we ended up at your brother's apartment. Basically, that letter and the following one did come from there, both written on his writing paper, with the letterhead carefully cut off.'

'I assume my brother set your mind at rest? This is Gus playing a practical joke, isn't it?'

'As far as I know, your nephew isn't in the habit of play-ing practical jokes.'

'No, you're right. And neither is Bambi. I don't know, could it be the young Swiss he hired as his office boy? Or the maid?'

'I've just received a third letter, this time by express mail, telling me that it's going to happen very soon.'

The doctor's tone had changed.

'Do you believe that?'

'I've only known the family since yesterday.'

'What does Émile say? I assume he shrugs it off?'

'Actually, he doesn't take it as lightly as that. On the contrary, I have the impression he believes there's a real threat.'

'A threat to whom?'

'Perhaps to himself.'

'Who would ever think of harming him? And why? Apart from his passion for revising Article 64, he's the most harmless and amiable person in the world.'

'He certainly won me over . . . You just used the word passion, doctor. As a neurologist, would you go so far as to call it an obsession?'

'In the medical sense of the term, certainly not.'

He had become more abrupt, having grasped Maigret's ulterior motive.

'What you're asking me is if I consider my brother to be of sound mind.'

'I wouldn't go that far.'

'Are you keeping the apartment under guard?'

'I've already sent one of my inspectors.'

'Has my brother had dealings with any suspicious people lately? Has he got in the way of someone with a lot of money?'

'He didn't tell me anything about his business affairs. But I know that, just this afternoon, he had two shipowners in his office, one Greek and one Dutch.'

'Yes, they come from as far away as Japan . . . Well, we just have to hope it's nothing but a hoax. Did you have any other questions you wanted to ask me?'

He was forced to improvise. At the other end, the neurologist was probably looking out at Promenade des Anglais and the blue waters of the Baie des Anges.

'Do you think your sister-in-law is a stable person?'

'Between ourselves – and of course I wouldn't repeat this in the witness box – if all women were like her, I'd have stayed a bachelor.'

'I asked you if she was stable.'

'Yes, I understood that. Let's just say that she's always going to extremes. And to be fair, let's also admit that it hurts her as much as it hurts anyone else.'

'Is she the kind of woman to become obsessed?'

'Of course, provided these obsessions have a basis in fact and are plausible. I'm certain that if she lied to you, her lie was so perfect that you didn't even notice it.'

'Would you use the word hysteria?'

There was quite a long silence.

'I wouldn't dare go that far, although I have occasionally seen her in a state that could be described as hysterical. The thing is, even though she's highly strung, she somehow, by some miracle or other, finds the strength to control herself.'

'Did you know she has a gun in her room?'

'Yes, she told me about it one evening. She even showed it to me. It's not much more than a toy.'

'A toy that can kill. Would you let her keep it in her drawer?'

'You know, if she ever decided to kill someone, she'd do it anyway, with or without a firearm.'

'Your brother also has a gun.'

'I know.'

'Would you say the same thing about him?'

'No. I'm convinced, not only as a man, but as a doctor, that my brother will never kill anyone. The only thing that might happen, one evening when he's feeling discouraged, would be that he would put an end to his own life.'

His voice had cracked.

'You love him very much, don't you?'

'There's just the two of us.'

The words struck Maigret. They still had their father, and Germain Parendon was also married. And yet he'd said:

'There's just the two of us.'

As if they only had each other in the world. Was the brother's marriage also a failed marriage?

Having probably checked the time, Dr Parendon snapped out of it.

'Well, let's hope nothing happens. Have a good evening, Monsieur Maigret.'

'You, too, Monsieur Parendon.'

Maigret had made the call to reassure himself. But the result had been quite the opposite. After talking to Émile Parendon's brother, he felt even more worried.

. . . The only thing that might happen, one evening when he's feeling discouraged . . .

Could that be what was brewing? Could it be Parendon himself who had written the anonymous letters? To stop himself from going ahead with it? To put a kind of barrier between the impulse and the act that tempted him?

Maigret had forgotten all about Janvier, who had gone to stand by the window.

'Did you hear?'

'What you said, yes.'

'He doesn't like his sister-in-law. He's convinced his brother will never kill anyone, but isn't so certain he won't be tempted to kill himself one of these days.'

The sun had disappeared, and it was suddenly as if something was missing from the world. It wasn't night yet. There was no point putting the lights on. Maigret did so anyway, as if to chase away ghosts.

'Tomorrow, you'll see the place and you'll start to understand. There's nothing to stop you from ringing the bell, telling Ferdinand who you are and wandering around the apartment and the offices. They've been informed. They're expecting it. The only thing you risk is seeing Madame Parendon suddenly appear when you're least expecting it. It's as if she's able to move around without displacing any air. She'll look at you, and you'll feel vaguely guilty. That's the impression she makes on everyone.'

Maigret called the office boy and gave him the signed documents and the mail that needed sending.

'Anything new? Anyone for me?'

'No, nobody, sir.'

Maigret wasn't expecting visitors. He was struck nevertheless that neither Gus nor his sister had come forward at any time. Like the rest of the household, they must know what had been happening since the day before. They had certainly heard that Maigret was questioning people. They might even have caught sight of him in the corridor.

If, at the age of fifteen, Maigret had heard that . . .

Of course he would have run to the police officer and bombarded him with questions, even if it meant being put in his place.

He realized that time had passed, that this was a different world.

'Shall we have a drink at the Brasserie Dauphine before we head off home for dinner?'

Which was what they did. Maigret walked for quite a while before taking a taxi, and by the time his wife, hearing his footsteps, opened the door, he didn't look too anxious.

'What's for dinner?'

'I've heated up the lunch.'

'And what was for lunch?'

'Cassoulet.'

They both smiled, but she had nevertheless guessed his mood.

'Don't worry, Maigret.'

He hadn't told her anything about the case he was dealing with. But then, weren't all cases the same?

'You're not responsible.'

After a moment, she added:

'At this time of year, it can turn cold quite suddenly. I'd
better shut the window.'

5.

As on other mornings, his first contact with life was the smell of coffee, then his wife's hand touching him on the shoulder, and finally the sight of Madame Maigret, already fresh and alert in a flowered house dress, handing him the cup.

He rubbed his eyes and asked quite stupidly:

'Have there been any telephone calls?'

If there had been any, they would have woken him as well as her. The curtains were open. The spring, premature as it was, remained fair. The sun had risen, and the noises of the street were clearly audible.

He heaved a sigh of relief. Lapointe hadn't called him. That meant that nothing had happened in the apartment on Avenue Marigny. He drank half his coffee, got up, feeling cheerful, and went into the bathroom. He had worried unduly. As soon as the first letter had arrived, he should have realized that it wasn't serious. This morning, he felt a little ashamed at having let it spook him. He had been like a child who still believes in ghost stories.

'Did you sleep well?'

'I slept wonderfully.'

'Do you think you'll be home for lunch?'

'This morning, I have the feeling I will.'

'Would you like fish?'

'Ray in brown sauce, if you can find it.'

He was surprised, embarrassed even, when he opened the door to his office half an hour later and found Lapointe sitting in an armchair. The poor boy was a little pale and drowsy. Rather than leaving his report and going to bed, he had preferred to wait for him, presumably because Maigret had seemed so worried the day before.

'Well, young man?'

Lapointe had got to his feet. Maigret sat down in front of the pile of mail on his desk.

'Just a moment . . .'

He wanted to make sure first that there wasn't another anonymous letter.

'Fine! Go ahead.'

'I got there just before six o'clock and made contact with Lamure, the concierge, who insisted on my having dinner with his wife and him. The first person who entered the building after me, at six ten, was the Parendon boy, the one they call Gus.'

Lapointe took a notebook from his pocket in order to refer to his notes.

'Was he alone?'

'Yes. He was holding a few school books under his arm. Then a few minutes later, an effeminate-looking man came in, holding a leather bag. Lamure told me he was the Peruvian woman's hairdresser. "There must be a gala or a big party somewhere," he said calmly as he knocked back his glass of cheap red wine . . . Incidentally, he got through a whole bottle by himself and was surprised, and even a bit annoyed, that I wouldn't do the same.

'Let's see, now . . . At seven forty-five, a woman arrived in a chauffeur-driven car. Madame Hortense, the concierge called her. She's one of Madame Parendon's sisters, the one who goes out with her most often. She's married to a Monsieur Benoît-Biguet, who's rich and important, and their chauffeur is Spanish.'

Lapointe smiled.

'Sorry, I know these details aren't very interesting, but since I didn't have anything to do, I noted everything down. At eight thirty, the Peruvians' limousine stopped under the archway, and the couple came out of the lift. He was wearing a suit, and she had an evening dress on under a chinchilla stole. Not the kind of thing you see very often these days.

'At eight fifty-five, Madame Parendon and Madame Hortense left. I found out later where they'd gone. When the chauffeurs get back, they usually come and have a drink in the lodge with Lamure, who always has a litre of red wine to hand . . . There was a charity bridge party at the Crillon, and that's where they went. They got back just after midnight. The sister went up and stayed up there for half an hour. That's when the chauffeur came and had his drink . . . Nobody paid any attention to me. They must have thought I was some friend or other. The hardest part was not having the drinks I was offered . . . Mademoiselle Parendon, the one they call Bambi, got back about one in the morning.'

'What time had she gone out?'

'I don't know. I didn't see her leave. That means she didn't have dinner at home. She was with a young man and she kissed him at the foot of the stairs. She didn't seem to care that we were there. I asked Lamure if she always did that. He said she did, and that it was always the same young man, but that he didn't know where he was from. He was wearing a jacket and shapeless moccasins, and his hair was quite long.'

His eyes on his notes, Lapointe seemed to be reciting, all the while fighting sleep.

'You haven't said anything about Mademoiselle Vague, Tortu or Julien Baud leaving.'

'Actually, I didn't make a note of it, because I assumed it was all part of the routine. They came down the stairs at six o'clock and separated once they were out on the street.'

'What else?'

'I went up to the fourth floor two or three times but didn't see or hear anything. I could just as well have been wandering around a church at night . . . The Peruvians came back about three in the morning after dinner at Maxim's and a film premiere on the Champs-Élysées. Apparently, they're well-known figures on the Paris scene . . . That's it for the night. Not a soul came in or out after that, not even a cat. Actually, there isn't a single pet in the building, apart from the Peruvians' parrot . . . Did I mention that Ferdinand, the Parendons' butler, went to bed about ten? Or that the cook left at nine?

'Ferdinand was the first to come out into the courtyard in the morning. That was at seven. He left the building because he's in the habit of going to the bar at the corner of Rue du Cirque to have his first coffee of the day with fresh croissants. He stayed out for half an hour. During that time, the cook arrived, and so did the cleaner, Madame Marchand. The chauffeur came down from his room, which is next to Ferdinand's, over the garages, and went upstairs for his breakfast . . .

'I didn't write everything down straight away. That's why my notes are in a bit of a mess. During the night, I went up about ten times and listened at the Parendons' door, but didn't hear anything . . . The Peruvians' chauffeur took out his employers' Rolls and washed it, as he does every morning . . .'

Lapointe put his notebook back in his pocket.

'That's all, chief. Janvier arrived. I introduced him to Lamure, though apparently Lamure already knew him, and left.'

'Now straight to bed with you, young man.'

In a few minutes, the bell for the daily briefing would echo through the corridors. Maigret filled a pipe, picked up his paper knife and quickly went through the mail.

He was relieved. He had every reason to be. All the same, he still had a knot in the pit of his stomach, a vague sense of apprehension.

In the commissioner's office, they talked mostly about a minister's son who had had a car accident on the corner of Rue François-Ier at four in the morning, in unpleasant circumstances. Not only had he been drunk, but it would cause a scandal if the name of the girl who had been with him and who had had to be taken to hospital was revealed. As for the driver of the car they had crashed into, he had died instantaneously.

'What do you think, Maigret?'

'Me? Nothing, sir.'

When it came to politics, or anything related to politics, Maigret ceased to exist. He was good at assuming a vague, almost stupid air.

'We have to find a solution, though. The press don't know anything about it for the moment, but they're bound to find out in an hour or two.'

It was ten o'clock. The telephone rang on the desk, and the commissioner nervously picked up the receiver.

'Yes, he's here.'

And, handing the receiver to Maigret:

'It's for you.'

He had a premonition. He knew, before lifting the receiver to his ear, that something had happened in the apartment on Avenue Marigny, and it was indeed Janvier's voice that he heard at the other end. It was low, almost embarrassed.

'Is that you, chief?'

'Yes. Who is it?'

Janvier immediately grasped the meaning of the question.

'The young secretary.'

'Dead?'

'Unfortunately.'

'Was she shot?'

'No. It happened without a sound. Nobody noticed anything. The doctor hasn't arrived yet. I'm calling you before I have any details because I was downstairs. Monsieur Parendon is with me now, he's devastated. We're expecting Dr Martin any moment.'

'Stabbed?'

'Her throat was cut.'

'I'll be right there.'

The commissioner and his colleagues were looking at him, surprised to see him looking so pale and so upset. At Quai des Orfèvres, especially in the crime squad, didn't they deal with murder on a daily basis?

'Who is it?' the commissioner asked.

'Parendon's secretary.'

'Parendon the neurologist?'

'No. His brother, the lawyer. I've been receiving anonymous letters . . .'

He rushed to the door without further explanation and went straight to the inspectors' room.

'Lucas?'

'Here, chief.'

He looked around.

'You, too, Torrence. Come into my office, both of you.'

Lucas, who knew about the letters, asked:

'Has the murder happened?'

'Yes.'

'Parendon?'

'The secretary. Phone Moers and tell him to get over there with his technicians. I'll call the prosecutor's office.'

It was always the same palaver. For a good hour, instead of working in peace, he was going to have to provide explanations to the deputy prosecutor and whichever examining magistrate was assigned to the case.

'Let's go, boys.'

He was overcome, as if this had happened to a family

member. Of all the people in the household, Mademoiselle Vague was the last one he would have thought of as a victim.

He had taken a liking to her. He liked the proud yet simple way she had spoken about her relationship with her employer. He had sensed that deep down, despite the difference in age, what she had felt for him was the kind of passionate loyalty that might well constitute one of the truest forms of love.

So why was she the one who had been killed?

He sank into the little black car while Lucas got in behind the wheel and Torrence took the back seat.

'What's this all about?' Torrence asked as they set off.

'You'll see soon enough,' Lucas replied, aware of Maigret's state of mind.

Maigret didn't see the streets, the people walking, the trees that were getting greener with each passing day, the big buses veering dangerously close to them.

He was already there, in the apartment. He pictured himself sitting by the window in Mademoiselle Vague's little office at this time yesterday. She was looking him straight in the face, as if to demonstrate the sincerity of her gaze. And whenever she hesitated after a question, it was because she was searching for the exact words.

There was already a car outside the door. It belonged to the chief inspector from the local station. Janvier must have alerted him. Because whatever happens, you have to follow the regulations.

Lamure was standing grim-faced in the doorway of his luxurious lodge.

'Who would have thought . . .' he began.

Maigret walked past him without replying. The lift being on one of the upper floors, he set off up the stairs. Janvier was waiting for him on the landing. He said nothing. He, too, could guess his chief's state of mind. Ferdinand was at his post, as if nothing had happened, but Maigret didn't even notice him taking his hat.

He set off along the corridor, passed the door of Parendon's office and came to the open door of Mademoiselle Vague's office. All he saw at first were two men, the local chief inspector, a man named Lambilliote, whom he had often met, and one of his colleagues.

He had to look down at the ground, almost under the Louis XIII table that served as a desk.

She was wearing an almond-green spring dress, presumably for the first time in the season: the previous day and the day before that he had seen her in a navy-blue skirt and a white blouse. It had struck him that it must be a kind of uniform for her.

After the attack, she must have slid off her chair. Her body was folded in on itself in a strangely twisted way. Her throat was open and she had lost a considerable amount of blood – it was probably still warm.

It took him a while to notice that Lambilliote was shaking his hand.

'Did you know her?'

He was looking at Maigret, astonished to see him so upset at the sight of a corpse.

'Yes, I knew her,' he said in a hoarse voice.

And he hurried to the office at the far end, where a

red-eyed Julien Baud loomed up in front of him. His breath smelled of alcohol. There was a bottle of cognac on the table. In his corner, René Tortu was holding his forehead in both hands.

'Was it you who found her?'

Maigret spontaneously adopted a gentle tone, because the tall Swiss suddenly looked like a little boy.

'Yes, monsieur.'

'Had you heard something? Did she cry out? Did she moan?'

'No, not at all.'

It was difficult for him to speak. He couldn't get rid of the knot in his throat, and tears streamed from his blue eyes.

'Forgive me. This is the first time . . .'

It was as if he had been waiting for this moment to start sobbing, and he took his handkerchief from his pocket.

'I . . . I'm sorry . . . Just a minute.'

He wept all the tears he had in him, standing in the middle of the room, looking taller than his one metre eighty. There was a sharp little noise. It was the tube of Maigret's pipe breaking under the pressure of his jaw. The bowl fell to the floor, and he bent down, picked it up and stuffed it in his pocket.

'I beg your pardon. I can't help myself.'

Baud caught his breath, wiped his eyes and glanced at the bottle of cognac, but didn't dare touch it again.

'She came in here about ten past nine to bring me some documents to collate. Actually, I can't remember where I put them. It was the transcript of yesterday's court session, with notes and references. I must have left them in her desk drawer . . . No, there they are! On my table.'

Crumpled by a nervous hand.

'She asked me to give them back to her as soon as I'd finished. I went to her office.'

'At what time?'

'I don't know. I must have worked for about thirty minutes . . . I was feeling quite cheerful, quite happy. I really like working for her . . . I looked in and didn't see her. Then I looked down . . .'

It was Maigret who poured a little cognac for him into the glass, which must have been brought by Ferdinand.

'Was she still breathing?'

He shook his head.

'The prosecutor's office, chief . . .'

'Did you hear anything, Monsieur Tortu?'

'No, nothing.'

'Were you here all the time?'

'No, I went to see Monsieur Parendon, and we spoke for about ten minutes about the case I was dealing with yesterday at the Palais.'

'What time was this?'

'I didn't look at my watch. About nine thirty.'

'How did he seem?'

'The same as usual.'

'Was he alone?'

'Mademoiselle Vague was with him.'

'Did she leave when you arrived?'

'A few moments later.'

Maigret would happily have had a swig of cognac, too,

but he didn't dare. The formalities awaited him. They annoyed him, but, when it came down to it, it wasn't a bad thing he would have to deal with them, because it forced him to break free of his nightmare.

The prosecutor's office had assigned Examining Magistrate Daumas, with whom he had worked several times, a pleasant, slightly shy man, probably in his forties, whose one defect was that he fussed over details. He was accompanied by Deputy Prosecutor De Claes, a tall, fair-haired man, very thin, dressed to the nines, who always held a pair of light-coloured gloves in his hand, winter and summer.

'What do you think, Maigret? I hear you had an inspector in the building? Were you expecting something like this to happen?'

Maigret shrugged and made a vague gesture.

'It's a long story. Yesterday and the day before, following some anonymous letters, I spent practically all my time in this apartment.'

'Did the letters say who the victim was going to be?'

'No, that's just it. That's why the murder was impossible to prevent. It would have needed an officer following each person here wherever they went in the apartment. Lapointe spent the night downstairs. This morning, Janvier came and relieved him.'

Janvier was standing in a corner, head bowed. From the courtyard, they could hear the jet of water as the Peruvians' chauffeur washed the Rolls.

'By the way, Janvier, who told you?'

'Ferdinand. He knew I was downstairs. I'd talked to him earlier.'

They heard heavy footsteps in the corridor. It was the technicians arriving with their equipment. A short, very round man had somehow got mixed up with them and he now looked at the people gathered in the room, wondering whom to address.

'Dr Martin,' he said eventually. 'I'm sorry I'm so late, I was with a patient, and it took her a long time to get dressed.'

He saw the body, opened his case and knelt on the wooden floor. He was the least upset of all of them.

'She's dead, of course.'

'Did she die immediately?'

'She probably survived for a few seconds, let's say thirty or forty. With her throat cut, there was no way she could cry out.'

He indicated an object partly hidden by the table: the sharp, pointed scalpel that Maigret had noticed the day before. It was now stuck in a pool of thick blood.

Maigret couldn't stop himself from looking at the woman's face, her glasses knocked sideways, her staring blue eyes.

'Would you mind closing her eyes, doctor?'

He hadn't often been so shaken by the sight of a corpse, except when he was starting out.

As the doctor was about to obey, Moers pulled him by the sleeve.

'The photographs,' he said.

'That's true. No, don't do anything.'

It was up to him to stop looking. They still had to wait for the pathologist. Dr Martin, who was very quick despite his paunch, asked:

'May I go, gentlemen?'

Then, looking at them in turn, he finally addressed Maigret.

'You're Inspector Maigret, aren't you? I wonder if I should go and see Monsieur Parendon. Do you know where he is?'

'In his office, I assume.'

'Does he know what's happened? Has he seen her?'

'Probably.'

Actually, nobody knew anything specific. There was a sense of incoherence in the air. A photographer was setting up a huge camera on a tripod while a grey-haired man was taking measurements on the floor and the examining magistrate's clerk was scribbling in a notebook.

Lucas and Torrence, who hadn't yet received any instructions, were standing in the corridor.

'What do you think I should do?'

'Go and see him if you think he might need you.'

Dr Martin had just got to the door when Maigret called him back.

'I'll probably have some questions to ask you during the day. Will you be in?'

'Except from eleven to one, when I have my clinic at the hospital.'

He took a large watch from his pocket, seemed unpleasantly surprised and walked away quickly.

Examining Magistrate Daumas coughed.

'I assume, Maigret, that you'd rather I left you to work in peace? I'd just like to know if you suspect anyone.'

'No . . . Yes . . . Frankly, sir, I don't know. This case isn't like most others, and I'm rather at sea.'

'Do you need me any more?' Lambilliote asked.

'No, I don't,' Maigret replied distractedly.

He couldn't wait for them all to go. The office gradually emptied. Occasionally a flash went off, even though the room was already bright. Two men were taking finger-prints of the dead woman, doing their job like carpenters or locksmiths.

Maigret slipped discreetly out of the room, made a sign to Lucas and Torrence to wait for him and went into the office at the far end, where Tortu was answering the phone while Baud sat with his elbows on his table, staring straight ahead.

He was drunk. The level of the cognac in the bottle had gone down by a good three fingers. Maigret grabbed it and shamelessly, because it really was necessary, poured some for himself into Baud's glass.

He was working like a sleepwalker, stopping occasionally, gaze fixed, afraid of forgetting something essential. He absently shook hands with the pathologist, whose real work would only begin at the Forensic Institute.

The men from the mortuary were already there with a stretcher, and he cast one last glance at the almond-green dress which should have marked a joyful spring day.

'Janvier, I'll leave you to deal with the parents. Their address should be in the office at the far end. Or look in her handbag. Anyway, do what you have to do.'

He led his other two colleagues towards the cloakroom.

'I want the two of you to make a plan of the apartment, question the staff, note down where each person was between nine fifteen and ten o'clock. Also note down what everyone saw, all their movements.'

Ferdinand was standing there, arms folded, waiting.

'He'll help you with the plan . . . Tell me, Ferdinand, I assume Madame Parendon is in her room?'

'Yes, Monsieur Maigret.'

'What was her reaction?'

'She hasn't had any reaction, monsieur. I don't think she knows anything yet. As far as I know, she's still asleep, and Lise didn't dare take the responsibility of waking her.'

'Hasn't Monsieur Parendon been to see her either?'

'Monsieur hasn't left his office.'

'So he hasn't seen the body?'

'I beg your pardon. He did actually come out briefly, when Monsieur Tortu went to tell him the news. He glanced into Mademoiselle Vague's office and then went back to his.'

The previous day, Maigret had been mistaken when, because his anonymous correspondent wrote so carefully, he had thought he should take the word *strike* literally.

She hadn't been struck. She hadn't been shot either. She had had her throat cut.

He had to stand aside to let the stretcher bearers pass. A few moments later, he was knocking at the monumental door of Parendon's office. He heard no answer. True, the door was of thick oak. He turned the handle, opened one half of the double door and saw the lawyer in one of the leather armchairs.

For a fraction of a second, he was afraid something might have happened to him, too, so hunched over was he, his chin on his chest, one flabby hand touching the rug.

Maigret stepped forwards and sat down in an armchair opposite him, so that they were now face to face, a short distance from one another, as they had been for their first interview. On the shelves, the names of Lagache, Henri Ey, Ruyssen and other psychiatrists glittered in gold lettering on the bindings.

He was surprised to hear a voice murmur:

'What do you think, Monsieur Maigret?'

The voice was distant, muffled. It was the voice of a devastated man, and Parendon barely made an effort to sit up and raise his head. As a result, his glasses fell to the floor, and without the thick lenses his eyes were those of a fearful child. He bent down with effort to pick them up and put them back on.

'What are they doing?' he asked, raising his white hand and pointing to his secretary's office.

'They've finished with the formalities.'

'What about the . . . the body?'

'It's just been taken away.'

'Don't mind me . . . I'll get a grip in a minute.'

With his right hand, he mechanically felt his heart. Maigret watched him as fixedly as on the first day.

He sat up now, took a handkerchief from his pocket and passed it over his face.

'Would you like a drink?'

His gaze moved to the part of the panelling that hid a small bar.

'What about you?'

Maigret took the opportunity to stand up and fetch two glasses and the bottle of old armagnac with which he was already familiar.

'It wasn't a joke,' Parendon said slowly.

And, although his voice had grown firmer, it was still strange, almost machine-like, toneless.

'This puts you in a difficult position, doesn't it?'

And, as Maigret was still looking at him without replying, he added:

'What are you going to do now?'

'Two of my men are busy checking the whereabouts of everyone here between nine fifteen and ten o'clock.'

'It was before ten o'clock.'

'I know.'

'Nine fifty. It was just nine fifty when Tortu came and told me.'

He glanced at the bronze clock, which showed 11.35.

'Have you been sitting in that armchair since then?'

'I followed Tortu down the corridor, but I couldn't bear the sight more than a few seconds . . . I came back here and . . . You're right, I haven't moved from this chair. I vaguely remember Martin, my doctor, coming in and speaking to me. I nodded, and he took my pulse and then left like a man in a hurry. He had to go to the hospital for his clinic. He must have thought I was drugged.'

'Have you ever taken drugs?'

'No, never . . . I can imagine the effect.'

Outside, the trees rustled slightly, and they could hear the din of buses on Place Beauvau.

'I would never have suspected . . .'

He was speaking incoherently, without finishing his sentences. Maigret still hadn't taken his eyes off him. He still had two pipes in his pocket, and he took out the one that wasn't broken, filled it and drew a few big puffs as if to put his feet back on the ground.

'Suspected what?'

'The point . . . The way . . . The importance . . . Yes, the importance, that's the word, of the connections . . .'

He again pointed towards his secretary's office.

'It's so unexpected!'

Would Maigret have felt surer of himself if he had absorbed all the works of psychiatry and psychology lined up on the shelves?

He couldn't remember having ever looked at a man with such intensity as he was doing now. He didn't want to miss one movement, one muscular quiver of the face.

'Had you thought it would be her?'

'No,' Maigret admitted.

'Me?'

'You or your wife.'

'Where is she?'

'Apparently she's asleep and doesn't know yet.'

Parendon frowned. He was making a great effort to concentrate.

'She never left her room?'

'Not according to Ferdinand.'

'That's not Ferdinand's department.'

'I know. One of my inspectors is probably questioning Lise right now.'

Parendon was starting to grow agitated, as if something he hadn't thought of before was suddenly nagging at him.

'So are you going to arrest me? I mean, if my wife didn't leave her room . . .'

Had he thought it so obvious that Madame Parendon was the killer?

'Well, are you?'

'It's too early to arrest anybody.'

Parendon stood up, took a gulp of the armagnac and wiped his forehead with the back of his hand.

'I don't understand what's going on any more, Maigret . . . I'm sorry – Monsieur Maigret,' he corrected himself. 'Did someone get into the apartment from outside?'

He was becoming himself again. Life had returned to his eyes.

'No. One of my men spent the night in the building, and another relieved him about eight this morning.'

'We need to reread the letters,' Parendon said in a low voice.

'I reread them several times yesterday afternoon.'

'There's something that doesn't hold together in all this. It's as if things suddenly happened that hadn't been planned.'

He sat down again, and Maigret pondered these words. He, too, when he had heard that Mademoiselle Vague was dead, had had the feeling it was a mistake.

'You know, she was very, very . . . devoted to me.'

'More than that,' Maigret said.

'Do you think so?'

'Yesterday she talked about you with genuine passion.'

Parendon opened his eyes wide, incredulous, as if he couldn't somehow convince himself that he had inspired such a feeling.

'I had a long conversation with her while you were seeing the two shipowners.'

'I know. She told me. What happened to the papers?'

'Julien Baud had them in his hand when he discovered the body and rushed back to his office in a panic. They're a bit crumpled.'

'They're very important. These people mustn't be allowed to suffer because of what happens here.'

'May I ask you a question, Monsieur Parendon?'

'I'd been expecting it since you came in. It's your duty to ask, of course, and even not to take me at my word. No, I didn't kill Mademoiselle Vague . . . There are words I haven't spoken often in my life, words I've almost erased from my vocabulary. Today, I'm going to use one of them, because it's the only one that expresses the truth I've just discovered. I loved her, Monsieur Maigret.'

He said this calmly, which made it all the more impressive. The rest was easier.

'I thought I was merely fond of her. That's in addition to the physical desire I felt, which I was almost ashamed of, because I have a daughter who's almost the same age as her. There was something about Antoinette . . .'

It was the first time Maigret had heard anyone use Mademoiselle Vague's first name.

'There was a kind of . . . what can I say? . . . a spontaneity I found refreshing . . . I mean, spontaneity isn't something you see a lot of in this household. She brought it in from outside, like a gift, like someone bringing freshly cut flowers.'

'Do you know what weapon was used for the murder?'

'A knife, I assume?'

'No, it was a kind of scalpel. I noticed it on your secretary's desk yesterday. I was struck by it, because it isn't the usual model. The blade is longer and sharper.'

'Like all our office supplies, it comes from Roman's Stationers.'

'Did you buy it?'

'Definitely not. She must have chosen it herself.'

'Mademoiselle Vague was sitting at her desk, probably examining documents. She'd given some of them to Julien Baud to collate.'

Parendon didn't look like a man on his guard, a man on the lookout for traps. He was listening attentively, a little surprised, perhaps, by the importance Maigret attached to these details.

'Whoever killed her knew they would find that scalpel in her pencil box, or they would have brought another weapon.'

'Isn't it possible they were armed but changed their mind?'

'Mademoiselle Vague saw the person take the scalpel and didn't react, didn't even stand up. She continued working while this person went behind her.'

Parendon was thinking, reconstructing in his mind – the mind of the great business lawyer that he was – the scene that Maigret had just described.

Nothing hesitant in his attitude. If you wanted to mock short people, you could call him a gnome, but he was a gnome of unusual intelligence.

'I think you're going to be obliged to arrest me before the day's out,' he said suddenly.

There was no sarcasm in this. He was a man who had weighed the pros and cons and come to a conclusion.

'It'll be an opportunity for my defence counsel,' he added, this time with a hint of irony, 'to practise the use of Article 64.'

Once again, Maigret was thrown. He was even more so when the door communicating with the large drawing room opened and they saw Madame Parendon in the doorway. She wore no make-up and hadn't done her hair. She was wearing the same blue dressing gown as the day before. She was standing very upright and yet she looked a lot older than her age.

'I'm sorry to disturb you.'

She spoke as if nothing had happened in the apartment.

'I don't suppose, inspector, that I'm allowed to have a private conversation with my husband? We don't often get the chance, but given the circumstances . . .'

'For the moment, I can only allow you to speak to him in my presence.'

She didn't advance into the room but stood where she was, with the sun-drenched drawing room behind her. The two men had got to their feet.

'Very well. You're only doing your job.'

She puffed at the cigarette she had in her hand and looked at them in turn, hesitantly.

'May I ask you first of all, Monsieur Maigret, if you've come to a decision?'

'A decision about what?'

'About what happened this morning. I've only just heard about it, and I suppose you'll be making an arrest.'

'I haven't come to a decision.'

'I see. The children will be back soon, and it's best for things to be clear. Tell me, Émile, was it you who killed her?'

Maigret couldn't believe his eyes or his ears. They were face to face, three metres apart, glaring at one another, their features tense.

'You dare ask me if . . .'

Parendon was choking, his little fists clenched with fury.

'No play-acting, please. Answer yes or no.'

All at once, he lost his temper, something that couldn't have happened often in his life. Raising both arms in a kind of plea to heaven, he cried:

'You know perfectly well I didn't, dammit!'

He was stamping his feet. He would have been quite capable of throwing himself at her.

'That's all I wanted to hear. Thank you.'

And with complete naturalness, she withdrew to the drawing room, closing the door behind her.

6.

'I'm sorry I flew off the handle, Monsieur Maigret. It's not like me.'

'I know.'

Maigret had become pensive for that very reason.

Parendon was still on his feet, catching his breath, recovering his composure and once again mopping his face, which wasn't red but yellowish.

'Do you hate her?'

'I don't hate anyone. Because I don't believe a human being is ever fully responsible.'

'Article 64!'

'Article 64, yes. I don't care if it makes me seem like a fanatic, I shan't change my opinion.'

'Even in the case of your wife?'

'Even in her case.'

'Even if she killed Mademoiselle Vague?'

For a moment, his face appeared to dissolve, the pupils to blur.

'Even then!'

'Do you think her capable of it?'

'I'm not accusing anyone.'

'I asked you a question earlier. I'm going to ask you another one, and you can answer yes or no. My anonymous correspondent isn't necessarily the murderer. Someone, sensing that a tragedy was imminent, may have imagined they would avoid it by bringing the police here.'

'I know what you're going to ask. No, I didn't write those letters.'

'Could it have been Mademoiselle Vague?'

He thought this over for a moment.

'It's not impossible. But it would have been out of character. She was more straightforward than that. I told you how spontaneous she was. She might not have told me directly, though, knowing perfectly well . . .'

He bit his lip.

'Knowing perfectly well what?'

'That if I'd felt threatened, I wouldn't have done anything about it.'

'Why not?'

He looked at Maigret and hesitated.

'It's hard to explain. I made my choice a long time ago.'

'Getting married?'

'Entering the career I chose. Getting married. Living in a certain way. So it's up to me to bear the consequences.'

'Isn't that contrary to your ideas about human responsibility?'

'Perhaps. On the surface, anyway.'

He seemed weary and helpless. Behind his bulging forehead, it was clear that he was trying hard to get his unruly thoughts into some kind of order.

'Do you believe, Monsieur Parendon, that the person who wrote to me thought the victim would be your secretary?'

'No.'

Out in the drawing room, in spite of the closed door, a voice could be heard crying:

'Where's my father?'

Then, almost immediately, the door was thrust open, and a very tall young man with tousled hair took two or three steps into the room and came to a halt in front of Maigret and Parendon.

His gaze went from one to the other and came to rest, almost threateningly, on Maigret.

'Are you planning to arrest my father?'

'Calm down, Gus. Inspector Maigret and I—'

'Are you Maigret?'

He looked at him with a greater degree of curiosity.

'Who are you going to arrest?'

'For the moment, nobody.'

'Anyway, I can swear to you that it wasn't my father.'

'Who told you what happened?'

'The concierge first, without going into any details, then Ferdinand.'

'Had you been expecting something like this?'

Parendon took the opportunity to go and sit down at his desk, as if to be back in his most habitual position.

'Is this an interrogation?'

The boy turned to his father as if to ask for advice.

'My role, Gus—'

'Who told you I'm called Gus?'

'Everyone in the household. I'm asking you questions, as I am everybody else, but this is not an official interrogation. I asked you if you had been expecting something like this.'

'Something like what?'

'Like what happened this morning.'

'If you mean was I expecting someone to cut Antoinette's throat, no.'

'You called her Antoinette?'

'Yes, always. We were good friends.'

'What had you been expecting?'

His ears abruptly turned red.

'Nothing in particular.'

'But something dramatic?'

'I don't know . . .'

Maigret noticed that Parendon was observing his son
with close attention, as if also asking himself a question,
or as if discovering something.

'You're fifteen, Gus, is that right?'

'I'll be sixteen in June.'

'Do you mind my talking to you in front of your father,
or would you rather we went into your bedroom or
another room?'

The boy hesitated. Although his excitement had subsided, he was still nervous. He again turned to his father.

'What would you rather I did, Father?'

'I think the two of you will be more comfortable in your
room . . . Hold on a moment, son. Your sister will be here
soon, if she isn't already. I'd like the two of you to have
lunch as usual without bothering about me. I won't be
coming to the table.'

'Aren't you eating?'

'I don't know. I may just have a sandwich. I need a little
peace and quiet.'

The boy looked as if he was ready to rush to his father and hug him, and it wasn't Maigret's presence that was stopping him, it was a reserve that had probably always existed between Parendon and his son.

They were neither of them inclined to outpourings of emotion, to hugs and kisses, and Maigret could easily imagine Gus, when he was younger, coming into his father's office and sitting there silent and motionless, watching him reading or working.

'If you want to come to my room, follow me.'

As they crossed the drawing room, Maigret found Lucas and Torrence waiting for him there, ill at ease in that vast, sumptuous room.

'Have you finished, boys?'

'All done, chief. Do you want to see the plan and hear about everyone's movements?'

'Not now. What time did it happen?'

'Between nine thirty and nine forty-five. Almost certainly nine thirty-seven.'

Maigret had turned to the wide-open windows.

'Were they open this morning?' he asked.

'From eight fifteen.'

Above the garages, the many windows of a six-storey building in Rue du Cirque were visible. It was the back of an apartment block. A woman was walking across a kitchen with a saucepan in her hand. On the third floor, another woman was changing a baby's nappy.

'Go and have something to eat, the two of you. Where's Janvier?'

'He's located the mother. She lives in a village in the

Berry. She doesn't have a phone, and he's asked someone there to bring her to where there is one. He's waiting for the call in the office at the end of the corridor.'

'Get him to join you for lunch. There's a restaurant in Rue de Miromesnil called Au Petit Chaudron that's not bad. Then divide up the floors of the buildings you can see over there in Rue du Cirque. Question the tenants whose windows look out on this side. For instance, they might have seen someone walking across the drawing room between nine thirty and nine forty-five. They probably look down into other rooms, too.'

'Where will you be?'

'At headquarters by the time you've finished. Unless you find out anything important. I may still be here.'

Gus was waiting, listening with interest. The drama that had occurred didn't stop him from still having a certain slightly childish curiosity about the police.

'I'm all yours, Gus.'

Walking along a corridor that was narrower than the one in the left wing, they passed a kitchen. Through the glass door, they could see a fat woman in dark clothes.

'It's the second door.'

The room was large, its atmosphere different from the rest of the apartment. Although the furniture was still period, presumably because they had wanted to find a use for it, Gus had changed its character by cluttering it with objects of all kinds and adding shelves and work benches.

There were four loudspeakers, two or three turntables, a microscope on a white wooden table, copper wires fixed to another table to form a complicated circuit. A single armchair by the window, over which a length of red cotton had been flung haphazardly. Red cotton also covered the bed, transforming it vaguely into a divan.

'You've kept this?' Maigret remarked, pointing to a large teddy bear on a shelf.

'Why should I be ashamed to? My father gave it to me on my first birthday.'

He uttered the word 'father' with pride, even defiance. He seemed ready to defend him fiercely.

'Did you like Mademoiselle Vague, Gus?'

'I already told you. We were friends.'

He must have been flattered that a twenty-five-year-old woman treated him as a friend.

'Did you often go to her office?'

'At least once a day.'

'Did you ever go out with her?'

The boy looked at him with surprise. Maigret was filling his pipe.

'Go out where?'

'The cinema, for instance. Or dancing.'

'I don't dance. No, I never went out with her.'

'Did you ever go to her apartment?'

His ears turned red again.

'What are you trying to make me say? What are you implying?'

'Did you know about Antoinette's relationship with your father?'

'Why not?' he retorted, head held high. 'Do you see any harm in it?'

'I'm not talking about me, I'm talking about you.'

'My father's free, isn't he?'

'What about your mother?'

'It was none of her business.'

'What exactly do you mean?'

'I mean a man has a perfect right . . .'

He didn't finish the sentence, but the beginning was explicit enough.

'Do you think that was the cause of the tragedy that occurred this morning?'

'I don't know.'

'Were you expecting a tragedy?'

Maigret had sat down in the red armchair and was slowly lighting his pipe, looking at this growing boy whose arms seemed too long, his hands too big.

'I'd been expecting it without expecting it.'

'Can you explain that a bit more clearly? I don't think your teacher at the Lycée Racine would accept an answer like that.'

'I never imagined you'd be like this.'

'Do you think I'm being hard on you?'

'Anyone would think you don't like me, or that you suspect me of something.'

'That's right.'

'Not of killing Antoinette, I hope? First of all, I was at school.'

'I know. I also know that you practically worship your father.'

'Is that a bad thing?'

'Not at all. At the same time, you think of him as a man who's defenceless.'

'What are you trying to insinuate?'

'Nothing bad, Gus. Your father, except perhaps in business, is inclined not to fight. He thinks that whatever happens to him is probably his fault.'

'He's an intelligent, conscientious man.'

'Antoinette was defenceless, too, in her way. Basically, there were two of you, she and you, watching over your father. That's why a degree of complicity sprang up between you.'

'We never talked about anything.'

'I can quite believe that. Nevertheless, you felt you were on the same side. That's why you never missed an opportunity to make contact with her even when you had nothing to say to her.'

'What are you getting at?'

For the first time, the young man, who had been fiddling with a copper wire, turned his head away.

'What I'm getting at is this. It was you, Gus, who sent me those letters and it was you who phoned the Police Judiciaire yesterday.'

Maigret could only see him from the back now. There was a long wait. At last, the boy turned to look at him, grim-faced.

'Yes, it was me. You'd have worked it out in the end anyway, wouldn't you?'

He was no longer looking at Maigret with the same defiance. Quite the contrary: Maigret had just risen in his esteem.

'What made you suspect me?'

'The letters could only have been written by the killer

or by someone who was trying indirectly to protect your father.'

'It could have been Antoinette.'

Maigret preferred not to reply that the secretary had been older than him and wouldn't have employed such a complicated – or such a childish – procedure.

'Have I disappointed you, Gus?'

'I thought you'd go about it in a different way.'

'How, for instance?'

'I don't know. I've read about your investigations. I thought of you as a man capable of understanding everything.'

'And now?'

He shrugged.

'Now I don't have an opinion.'

'Who would you have liked me to arrest?'

'I didn't want you to arrest anybody.'

'Then what was I supposed to do?'

'You're the one in charge of the crime squad, not me.'

'Had a crime already been committed yesterday, or even this morning at nine o'clock?'

'Of course not.'

'Then what were you trying to protect your father from?'

There was another silence.

'I sensed that he was in danger.'

'What kind of danger?'

Maigret was convinced that Gus understood the meaning of his question. The boy had wanted to protect his father. From whom? Couldn't it just as easily have been to protect him from himself?

'I don't want to answer any more questions.'

'Why?'

'I just don't want to!'

He added, resolutely:

'You can take me to Quai des Orfèvres, if you like, and ask me the same questions for hours. You may think I'm just a child, but I swear to you I won't say anything more.'

'I'm not asking you any more questions. It's lunchtime, Gus.'

'It doesn't matter if I get back to school late today.'

'Where's your sister's room?'

'Two doors further down, on the same corridor.'

'No hard feelings?'

'You're doing your job.'

Gus slammed the door once Maigret had gone out. Behind Bambi's door, the sound of a vacuum cleaner could be heard. Maigret knocked, and a young girl in uniform, with very fair, very loose hair, opened.

'Are you looking for me?'

'Is your name Lise?'

'Yes. I'm the maid. You've already passed me in the corridors.'

'Where's mademoiselle?'

'She could be in the dining room. Or with her father or mother. They're in the other wing.'

'I know. I went to see Madame Parendon there yesterday.'

Through an open door, he could see a dining room, wood-panelled from floor to ceiling. The table had been laid for two, although it could easily seat twenty. Soon,

Bambi and her brother would be here, separated by a vast expanse of tablecloth and waited on by Ferdinand, stiff in his white cotton gloves.

In passing, he half opened the door to Parendon's office. Parendon was sitting in the same armchair as this morning. On a folding table, there were a bottle of wine, a glass and a few sandwiches. Parendon didn't move. Had he even heard? There was a patch of sunlight on his cranium, which gave the impression he was bald.

Maigret closed the door again, found the corridor he had walked along the day before and reached the door to the boudoir. Through this, he heard a vehement, tragic voice which he didn't know.

He couldn't make out the words, but there was no mistaking the fury in them.

He knocked loudly. The voice broke off abruptly, and a moment later the door opened and a young woman stood there, still panting, her eyes bright, her breathing laboured.

'What do you want?'

Behind her stood Madame Parendon, still in her blue dressing gown. She had turned towards the window, hiding her face from him.

'I'm Detective Chief Inspector Maigret.'

'I suspected as much. So what? Have we lost the right to be here in our own home?'

She wasn't beautiful, but she had a pleasant face and a well-proportioned body. She was wearing a simple tailored suit, and her hair was held in place, unfashionably, with a ribbon.

'I was hoping to have a few words with you, mademoiselle, before you go to lunch.'

'Here?'

He had seen Madame Parendon's shoulders quiver.

'Not necessarily. Wherever you like.'

Bambi left the room without looking behind her, closed the door and said:

'Where would you prefer?'

'Your room?' he suggested.

'Lise's busy doing my room.'

'One of the offices?'

'I don't mind.'

Her hostility wasn't directed specifically at Maigret. It was more of a mood. Now that her violent harangue had been cut short, her excitement subsided, and she followed him wearily.

'Not in . . .' she began.

Not in Mademoiselle Vague's office, of course. They entered the office shared by Tortu and Julien Baud, who had both gone to lunch.

'Have you seen your father? . . . Please sit down.'

'I prefer to stand.'

She was still too nervous to sit on a chair.

'Whatever you prefer.'

He didn't sit down either, but leaned on Tortu's desk.

'I asked you if you'd seen your father.'

'Not since I got back, no.'

'When did you get back?'

'At a quarter past twelve.'

'Who told you what had happened?'

'The concierge.'

Lamure seemed to have watched out for the two of them, Gus and his sister, so as to be the first to break the news.

'And then?'

'Then what?'

'What did you do?'

'Ferdinand tried to speak to me, but I didn't listen to him. I went straight to my room.'

'Did you find Lise there?'

'Yes. She was cleaning the bathroom. Because of what happened, everything's late.'

'Did you cry?'

'No.'

'Didn't it occur to you to go and see your father?'

'Maybe. I don't remember. I didn't go.'

'Did you stay in your room for a long time?'

'I didn't look at the time. Five minutes or a little more.'

'Doing what?'

She looked at him and hesitated. It seemed to be a habit in this household. They all had a tendency to weigh their words before speaking.

'Looking at myself in the mirror.'

She was being defiant. That was another characteristic of this family.

'Why?'

'You want me to be honest, don't you? Well, I will be! I was trying to figure out who I look like.'

'You mean, your father or your mother?'

'Yes.'

'And what conclusion did you come to?'

She grew sterner.

'My mother!' she said angrily.

'Do you hate your mother, Mademoiselle Parendon?'

'I don't hate her. I'd like to help her. I've often tried.'

'Help her to do what?'

'Do you think this is leading anywhere?'

'What are you talking about?'

'Your questions . . . My answers . . .'

'They might help me to understand.'

'You spend a few odd hours with a family, and you claim you can understand? Don't think I'm hostile to you. I know you've been prowling around the place since Monday.'

'Do you also know who sent me the letters?'

'Yes.'

'How did you find out?'

'I caught him cutting pieces of paper.'

'Did Gus tell you what he was doing that for?'

'No. It was only later, when people started talking about the letters, that I put two and two together.'

'Who told you about them?'

'I can't remember. Maybe Julien Baud. I like him. He looks like a freak, but he's a nice boy.'

'I'm intrigued by something. It was you, wasn't it, who chose the nickname Bambi for yourself and Gus for your brother?'

She looked at him with a slight smile.

'Does that surprise you?'

'Was it a protest?'

'You guessed right. A protest against this big, solemn apartment, against the way we live, against the people who come here. I wish I'd been born in a modest family and had to struggle to make my way in life.'

'You are struggling, in your way.'

'Oh, yes, archaeology. I didn't want a career where I would have taken someone's place.'

'It's your mother who annoys you the most, isn't it?'

'I'd really rather not talk about her.'

'Unfortunately, she's the one who matters right now, isn't she?'

'Maybe . . . I don't know . . .'

She stole a glance at him.

'You think she's guilty,' Maigret insisted.

'What makes you say that?'

'When I went to the boudoir, I heard you speaking very angrily.'

'That doesn't mean I think she's guilty. I don't like the way she behaves. I don't like the life she leads, the life she makes us lead. I don't like . . .'

She was less good than her brother at controlling herself, even though she was apparently calmer.

'Do you blame her for not making your father happy?'

'You can't make people happy if they don't want to be. But when it comes to making them unhappy . . .'

'Did you like Mademoiselle Vague as much as you like Julien Baud?'

She didn't hesitate for a second.

'No!'

'Why not?'

'Because she was a little schemer who convinced my father that she loved him.'

'Did you ever hear them talk about love?'

'Obviously not. She wasn't going to bill and coo in front of me. You just had to see her when she was with him. I know exactly what happened once the door was closed.'

'Are you speaking from a moral standpoint or—'

'I don't give a damn about morals. Whose morals anyway? The morals of which social class? Do you think this neighbourhood has the same morals as a little provincial town, or the twentieth arrondissement?'

'In your opinion, did she make your father suffer?'

'Maybe she isolated him more.'

'You mean she distanced him from you?'

'These are questions I haven't thought about, that nobody thinks about. Let's just say that if she hadn't come along, there might have been a chance.'

'A chance for what? For things to be patched up?'

'There was nothing to patch up. My parents have never loved each other. Not that I believe in love anyway. But there's always the possibility of living in peace, in some kind of harmony.'

'Is that what you tried to bring about?'

'I tried to get my mother to calm down, to be more reasonable.'

'Didn't your father help you?'

She didn't think the same way as her brother and yet, on a small number of points, she had the same ideas.

'My father had given up.'

'Because of his secretary?'

'I'd rather not answer that. I've had enough of talking. Put yourself in my place. I get back from the Sorbonne and find—'

'You're right. All I'm trying to do, believe me, is cause the least possible upset. Imagine an investigation that drags on for weeks, the uncertainty, being summoned to the Police Judiciaire, then to the examining magistrate's office . . .'

'I hadn't thought of that. What are you going to do?'

'I haven't decided yet.'

'Have you had lunch?'

'No. Neither have you, and your brother's probably waiting for you in the dining room.'

'Is my father having lunch with us?'

'He'd rather be alone in his office.'

'What about you? Aren't you having lunch?'

'I'm not hungry for the moment, but I must confess I'm dying of thirst.'

'What would you like to drink? Beer? Wine?'

'Anything, as long as it's a big glass.'

She couldn't help smiling.

'Wait a moment.'

He had understood her smile. She couldn't see him going to the kitchen or the servants' hall for a drink, like a delivery boy. Nor could she imagine him sitting down with Gus and her in the dining room while they had lunch in silence.

When she returned, she hadn't burdened herself with a tray. In one hand, she held a bottle of six-year-old Saint-Émilion, in the other, a cut crystal glass.

'I'm sorry if I answered your questions so curtly, or if I haven't been very helpful.'

'You've all been very helpful. Now go and have your lunch, Mademoiselle Bambi.'

It was a strange sensation being there, at one end of the apartment, in the office shared by Tortu and the young Swiss, alone with a bottle and a glass. Because he had mentioned a large glass, she had chosen a water glass, and he wasn't ashamed to fill it.

He really was thirsty. He needed a pick-me-up, too, because this had been one of the most exhausting mornings of his career. And now he was sure that Madame Parendon was waiting for him. She couldn't be unaware that he had questioned everyone else in the household, and she must be fretting, wondering when he would finally get to her.

Had she sent for something to eat in her boudoir, the way her husband had done?

Standing at the window, he sipped his wine and looked out vaguely at the courtyard, which he was seeing for the first time empty of cars, with only a ginger cat stretching in a patch of sunlight. As Lamure had told Lapointe that there wasn't a single animal in the building apart from a parrot, it must have been a cat from the neighbourhood that had sought out a quiet spot.

He wondered whether he should pour himself another drink, finally poured half a glass, and waited until he had filled a pipe before drinking it.

After which, he heaved a sigh and headed for the boudoir, along the corridors he was by now familiar with.

He didn't need to knock. Despite the carpeting, his

footsteps had been heard, and the door opened as soon as he approached. Madame Parendon, still in her blue silk dressing gown, had had time to put on make-up and do her hair, and her face looked pretty much the same as it had the day before.

Did she look tenser or wearier? He would have been hard put to say. He sensed a difference, as if something had cracked, but he was unable to pinpoint what it was.

'I've been waiting for you.'

'I know. I'm here now, as you can see.'

'Why did you insist on seeing everybody else before me?'

'Perhaps it was to give you time to think.'

'I don't need to think. Think about what?'

'About what happened. About what's bound to happen next.'

'What are you talking about?'

'Whenever a murder is committed, it's followed, sooner or later, by an arrest, a legal process, a trial.'

'And how is that any concern of mine?'

'You hated Antoinette, didn't you?'

'So you also call her by her first name?'

'Who else does that here?'

'Gus, for example. My husband, I don't know. He's quite capable of politely saying "mademoiselle" while making love.'

'She's dead.'

'So what? Just because a person's dead, do we have to pretend they were a saint?'

'What did you do last night when your sister left after bringing you back from the Crillon?'

She frowned, then sniggered:

'I'd forgotten you'd stuck policemen everywhere . . . As it happens, I had a headache, I took an aspirin and tried to read while waiting for it to take effect. Look, the book's still there. You'll find a bookmark on page ten or twelve. I didn't get very far with it. I went to bed, but couldn't get to sleep. It happens to me quite often, my doctor knows all about it.'

'Dr Martin?'

'Dr Martin is my husband's doctor and the children's. My doctor is Dr Pommeroy, who lives on Boulevard Haussmann. I'm not ill, thank God!'

She uttered these words vigorously, almost defiantly.

'I don't follow any treatment, any diet.'

The subtext seemed to be:

'Unlike my husband.'

She didn't say that, but went on:

'The only thing I have to complain about is lack of sleep. Sometimes I'm still awake at three in the morning. It's exhausting and also painful.'

'Was that the case last night?'

'Yes.'

'Were you worried about something?'

'Your visit, you mean?' she retorted.

'You could have been worried about the anonymous letters, the atmosphere they created . . .'

'I haven't slept well for years, and that had nothing to do with any anonymous letters. Be that as it may, I finally got up and took a barbiturate that Dr Pommeroy had prescribed. If you want to see the box . . .'

'Why should I?'

'No idea. Judging by the questions you asked me yesterday, I suppose I should be prepared for anything . . . In spite of that sleeping pill, it still took me at least another half hour to fall asleep, and when I woke up I was amazed to see that it was eleven thirty.'

'I thought you often got up late.'

'Not as late as that. I rang for Lise, and she brought me a tray of tea and toast. It wasn't until she opened the windows that I realized her eyes were red. I asked her why she'd been crying. She burst into tears again and told me something terrible had happened. My first thought was that it was my husband.'

'What did you think had happened to him?'

'Do you think he's a strong person? Don't you think his heart could give out at any moment, like everything else?'

He didn't pick her up on the words 'like everything else', deciding to keep that for later.

'In the end she told me that Mademoiselle Vague had been killed and that the house was full of policemen.'

'What was your first reaction?'

'I was so astounded that at first I just drank my tea . . . Then I rushed to my husband's office. What are they going to do with him?'

He pretended he didn't understand.

'With whom?'

'My husband. You're not going to throw him in prison, are you? With his health . . .'

'Why would I put your husband in prison? First of all, it's not up to me, it's up to the examining magistrate.

Secondly, I don't see any reason at this stage to arrest your husband.'

'Who do you suspect, then?'

He didn't reply. He walked slowly up and down on the blue carpet with its yellow leaf pattern, while she settled herself in the wing chair that she had sat in the day before.

'Madame Parendon,' he asked, speaking slowly and clearly, 'why would your husband have killed his secretary?'

'Does there have to be a reason?'

'People don't usually commit murder without a motive.'

'Some people may invent an imaginary motive, don't you think?'

'And what would that be in this case?'

'What if she was pregnant, for example?'

'Do you have any reason to believe she was pregnant?'

'None at all.'

'Is your husband a Catholic?'

'No.'

'Then if she was pregnant, it's quite likely he'd have been delighted.'

'It would have complicated his life.'

'You forget we're no longer in the days when unmarried mothers were pointed at in the street. Times change, Madame Parendon. There are also lots of people who wouldn't hesitate to turn to a broad-minded gynaecologist.'

'I only mentioned it as an example.'

'Give me another one.'

'She might have been blackmailing him.'

'About what? Is there something shady in your husband's business affairs? Do you think he's capable of committing the kind of irregularities that might tarnish his reputation as a lawyer?'

She was forced to give up and say:

'Certainly not.'

She lit a cigarette.

'These girls always end up trying to get themselves married.'

'Has your husband ever mentioned divorce?'

'Not so far.'

'What would you do if he did?'

'I'd be obliged to resign myself and stop looking after him.'

'I believe you have a personal fortune?'

'Yes, and it's larger than his. This is my apartment. In fact, I own the building.'

'Then I see no reason for blackmail.'

'It's also possible to get tired of a false love.'

'Why false?'

'Because of age, background, lifestyle, whatever.'

'Is your love truer?'

'I gave him two children.'

'You mean you included them as part of the dowry?'

'Are you insulting me?'

She gave him another angry look, while he remained exaggeratedly calm.

'That isn't my intention, madame, but it usually takes two to make children. Why don't you just say that you and your husband had two children together?'

'What are you getting at?'

'I'd like you to tell me, quite simply and quite honestly, what you did this morning.'

'I've already told you.'

'Not simply, and not honestly. You told me a long story about insomnia and then skipped the whole morning.'

'I was asleep.'

'I'd like to be sure of that. It's likely that I'll know within quite a short time. My inspectors have noted the where-abouts and movements of everyone between nine fifteen and ten o'clock. I'm also aware that there are different ways of getting into the offices.'

'Are you accusing me of lying?'

'I'm accusing you of not telling me the whole truth.'

'Do you think my husband is innocent?'

'I don't prejudge anyone's innocence, just as I don't pre-judge anyone's guilt.'

'And yet the way you're interrogating me . . .'

'What was your daughter accusing you of when I came looking for her?'

'Didn't she tell you?'

'I didn't ask her.'

Once again, she sniggered, curling her lips in a bitter, ironic grin that was deliberately cruel and contemptuous.

'She's luckier than I am.'

'I asked you what she was accusing you of.'

'For not being with her father at a moment like this, if you really must know.'

'Does she think her father is guilty?'

'What if she does?'

'Gus, too, I suppose?'

'Gus is still at an age when his father's some kind of god and his mother's a shrew.'

'Earlier, when you came to your husband's office, you knew you would find me there with him.'

'You aren't necessarily everywhere, Monsieur Maigret, and I might have hoped to find my husband alone.'

'You asked him a question.'

'A perfectly simple, perfectly natural question, the question any wife would have asked in the circumstances. You saw his reaction. Do you think it was normal? Do you think a normal man would have started stamping his feet and stammering insults?'

Sensing that she had just scored a point, she lit another cigarette, having stubbed out the first one in a blue marble ashtray.

'I'm waiting for your other questions, if you still have any to ask me.'

'Have you had lunch?'

'Don't worry about that. If you're hungry . . .'

Her face was capable of changing from one minute to the next, and so was her demeanour. She was once again very much a woman of the world. Sitting back slightly in her chair, her eyes half closed, she was taunting him.

7.

Ever since the beginning of his interview with Madame Parendon, Maigret had been controlling himself. And gradually sadness had prevailed over irritation. He felt heavy, awkward; he realized all the things he didn't know and ought to know if he was going to bring such an interrogation to a conclusion.

He finally sat down in one of the armchairs that were too fragile for him, his pipe extinguished in his hand, and said in a calm but flat voice:

'Listen to me, madame. Contrary to what you may think, I'm not hostile to you. I'm merely a public servant whose job is to look for the truth by the means at his disposal. I'm going to ask you again the question I asked you earlier. I'd like you to think before you answer, to weigh up the pros and cons. I warn you that if, subsequently, it's proved that you've lied, I'll draw my own conclusions and ask the examining magistrate for a summons.'

He was observing her, especially her hands, which betrayed her inner tension.

'Since nine o'clock this morning, have you left your room and your boudoir and gone to the offices, for whatever reason?'

She didn't flinch, didn't turn her eyes away. As he had asked her to, she took her time, but it was clear that she wasn't thinking, that her position had been fixed once and for all. Finally she said:

'No.'

'You didn't go along the corridors?'

'No.'

'You didn't walk across the drawing room?'

'No.'

'You didn't go into Mademoiselle Vague's office, even on the spur of the moment?'

'No. I should add that I consider these questions insulting.'

'It's my duty to ask them.'

'You forget that my father is still alive.'

'Is that a threat?'

'I'm simply reminding you that you're not in your office at Quai des Orfèvres.'

'Would you rather I took you there?'

'I challenge you to do so.'

He preferred not to take her at her word. When he was at Meung-sur-Loire, he sometimes went fishing. He had once caught an eel and had then had the devil's own job getting it off the hook. It had constantly slid from his fingers and had finally fallen into the grass on the river bank, from where it had slithered back into the water.

He wasn't here for his pleasure. He wasn't fishing.

'Do you deny that you killed Mademoiselle Vague?'

The same words, constantly, the same look in his eyes, that of a man trying desperately to understand another human being.

'You know perfectly well.'

'What do I know?'

'That it's my poor husband who killed her.'

'For what reason?'

'I told you. As things stand, there's no need for a specific reason. I'm going to tell you something that only he and I know, something he confided in me before we got married. He was scared of getting married. He kept putting it off. What I didn't know at the time was that he'd been seeing a number of different doctors . . . Did you know that when he was seventeen he tried to kill himself because he was afraid he wasn't a normal man? He cut his wrists. When the blood spurted, he started to panic and called for help, claiming it was an accident . . . Do you know what this tendency to suicide means?'

Maigret was sorry he hadn't brought the bottle of wine with him. Tortu and Julien Baud must have been surprised to find it in their office when they got back and had probably already finished it.

'He had qualms . . . he was afraid our children wouldn't be normal. When Bambi started to grow and talk, he would watch her anxiously.'

It might be true. There was certainly some truth in what she was saying, but he still sensed some discrepancy, a rift between the words, the sentences, and reality.

'He's haunted by a fear of sickness and death. Dr Martin knows all about it.'

'I saw Dr Martin this morning.'

She seemed to be thrown by this but quickly regained her composure.

'Didn't he tell you?'

'No. And he didn't think for a moment that your husband might be the murderer.'

'You're forgetting professional confidentiality, inspector.'

He was starting to glimpse a light, but it was still dim and distant.

'I also spoke to his brother on the phone. He's in Nice for a conference.'

'Is that after what happened?'

'No, before.'

'Was he upset?'

'He didn't advise me to keep an eye on your husband.'

'All the same, he must know.'

She lit yet another cigarette. She was chain-smoking them, inhaling deeply.

'Haven't you ever met people who've lost contact with life, with reality, and who somehow turn in on themselves, like a glove being turned inside out? Question our friends. Ask them if my husband still takes any interest in human beings. Every now and again, because I insist, he has dinner with a few people, but he barely notices they're there and only says a few words to them. He doesn't listen, just sits there all withdrawn.'

'Does he choose these friends you're talking about?'

'They're people we're duty bound to meet in our situation, normal people, living normal lives.'

He didn't ask her what she considered a normal life, preferring to let her speak. Her monologue was becoming increasingly instructive.

'Last summer, do you think he ever once put in an appearance at the beach or in the swimming pool? He spent his time in the garden, under a tree. When I was younger and he would suddenly stop listening to me, I assumed he was distracted. Now I think it's a genuine inability to live with other people. That's why he's always shut up in his office, why he hardly ever leaves it and when he does why he looks at us like an owl surprised by the light . . . You've rushed to judgement, Monsieur Maigret.'

'I have another question to ask you.'

He was sure of the answer in advance.

'Have you touched your revolver since last night?'

'Why should I have touched it?'

'I don't want a question from you, but an answer.'

'The answer is no.'

'When was the last time you handled it?'

'Months ago. I haven't tidied that drawer for ages.'

'You touched it yesterday, to show it to me.'

'I'd forgotten.'

'But when I took hold of it, my fingerprints may have got mixed up with the others.'

'Is that all you can come up with?'

She looked at him as if she was disappointed to discover that Maigret could be clumsy and flat-footed.

'You've just spoken quite smugly about your husband's isolation, his lack of contact with reality. And yet just yesterday, in his office, he was dealing with some extremely important business, and with men who definitely have both feet on the ground.'

'Why do you think he chose maritime law? He's never set foot on a ship in his life. He has no contact with sailors. It all happens on paper. It's all abstract, don't you understand? It's one more proof of what I've been telling you, of what you refuse to consider.'

She stood up and started walking around the room like someone thinking.

'Even his hobby horse, the famous Article 64. Isn't that proof that he's scared, scared of what he can do, and is trying to reassure himself? He knows you're here, he knows you're questioning me. In this house, nobody's unaware of everyone else's movements. Do you know what he's thinking? He's hoping I'll get impatient, that I'll seem nervous, that I'll lose my temper, and then I'll be a suspect instead of him. With me in prison, he'd be free.'

'Hold on a moment. I don't understand. What new freedom would he enjoy?'

'Total freedom.'

'What would he do with it, now that Mademoiselle Vague is dead?'

'There are other Mademoiselle Vagues.'

'So now you're claiming that your husband would take advantage of your absence to have mistresses?'

'Why not? It's another way of reassuring himself.'

'By killing them one after another?'

'He wouldn't necessarily kill the others.'

'I thought he was incapable of human contact.'

'With normal people, people from our world.'

'Because people who aren't from your world aren't normal?'

'You know perfectly well what I meant. I'm simply saying that it isn't normal for him to be involved with such people.'

'Why not?'

There was a knock at the door, and it opened to reveal Ferdinand in a white jacket.

'One of these gentlemen would like to talk to you, Monsieur Maigret.'

'Where is he?'

'Out here, in the corridor. He told me it's extremely urgent, and I took the liberty of bringing him.'

Maigret glimpsed Lucas in the gloom of the corridor.

'Will you excuse me a moment, Madame Parendon?'

He closed the door behind him, leaving her alone in her boudoir. Ferdinand walked away.

'What is it, Lucas?'

'She went across the drawing room twice this morning.'

'Are you sure?'

'You can't see him from here, but you can from the drawing room. There's an invalid who sits at one of the windows in Rue du Cirque almost all day.'

'Is he very old?'

'No, in his fifties. He had an accident and can't use his legs. He takes an interest in everything that goes on in this building. He's fascinated by the washing of the cars, especially the Rolls. Judging by his answers to some additional questions I asked him, I think we can trust his testimony. His name's Montagné. His daughter's a midwife.'

'What time did he first see her?'

'Just after nine thirty.'

'Was she going in the direction of the offices?'

'Yes. He's more familiar than we are with the layout of this place. That's how he knows about the relationship between Parendon and his secretary.'

'What was she wearing?'

'A blue dressing gown.'

'And the second time?'

'Less than five minutes later, she walked across the drawing room in the other direction. One thing he noticed was that the maid was at the far end of the room, doing the dusting, and she didn't see her.'

'Madame Parendon didn't see the maid?'

'No.'

'Have you questioned Lise?'

'This morning, yes.'

'Did she mention that?'

'She claims she didn't see anything.'

'Thanks, Lucas.'

'What should I do?'

'Wait for me, both of you. Any confirmation of what this Montagné said?'

'Only a maid on the fifth floor over there who thinks she saw something blue at the same time.'

Maigret knocked at the door of the boudoir and entered just as Madame Parendon was coming out of her bedroom. He took the time to empty his pipe and fill it.

'Would you be so kind as to call your maid?'

'Do you need something?'

'Yes.'

'As you wish.'

She pressed a button. A few moments passed in silence.

Looking at this woman he was torturing, Maigret couldn't help feeling a tightness in his chest.

He kept repeating to himself the text of Article 64, about which there had been so much talk here in the past three days:

> There is no crime or offence if the accused was in a state of insanity at the time of the act, or if he was compelled by a force he was unable to resist.

Could the man Madame Parendon had described to him, her husband, have acted in a state of insanity at a particular moment?

Had she, too, read books on psychiatry? Or else . . .

Lise entered, looking fearful.

'You called me, madame?'

'The inspector would like to talk to you.'

'Close the door, Lise. Don't be afraid. This morning, when you answered my inspectors, you were still in shock and probably didn't understand how important their questions were.'

The poor girl looked in turn at Maigret and at her mistress, who was again in the wing chair, sitting back, legs crossed, with an indifferent air as if none of this concerned her.

'It's quite possible you may have to testify in court, where you'll be under oath. You'll be asked the same questions. If it's established that you're lying, you'll incur a prison sentence.'

'I don't know what you're talking about.'

'We've established the whereabouts of all the members of staff between nine fifteen and ten o'clock. Just after nine thirty, you were dusting in the drawing room. Is that right?'

Another glance at Madame Parendon, who was avoiding looking at her, then, in a weak voice:

'Yes.'

'What time did you enter the drawing room?'

'About nine thirty, or just after.'

'So you didn't see Madame Parendon walking in the direction of the offices?'

'No.'

'But just after you started, when you were at the far end of the room, you saw her walk by in the opposite direction, in other words, towards this room.'

'What should I do, madame?'

'That's up to you, my girl. Answer the question you've been asked.'

Tears ran down Lise's cheeks. She had taken a handkerchief from the pocket of her apron and rolled it into a ball.

'Has someone told you something?' she asked Maigret innocently.

'Answer the question, as you've just been advised.'

'Will it get madame in trouble?'

'It'll confirm another testimony, the testimony of someone who lives in Rue du Cirque and saw both of you from his window.'

'Then there's no point in my lying. It's true. I'm sorry, madame.'

She made as if to rush to her mistress, perhaps to throw herself on her knees, but Madame Parendon said curtly:

'If the inspector has finished with you, that'll be all.'

Lise left the room, bursting into tears at the door.

'What does that prove?' Madame Parendon asked, back on her feet now, a cigarette quivering at her lips, her hands in the pockets of her blue dressing gown.

'That you've told at least one lie.'

'This is my home, and I don't have to give an account of my movements.'

'When there's a murder, you do. I did warn you when I asked the question.'

'Does this mean you're going to arrest me?'

'I'm going to ask you to come with me to Quai des Orfèvres.'

'Do you have a warrant?'

'I have a blank summons. I just have to write your name.'

'And then?'

'Then it will no longer depend on me.'

'Who will it depend on?'

'The examining magistrate. Then probably on the doctors.'

'Do you think I'm mad?'

He could see panic in her eyes.

'Answer me. Do you think I'm mad?'

'It's not for me to say.'

'I'm not mad, do you hear me? And, even if I did kill someone, which I continue to deny, it wasn't in a fit of madness.'

'May I ask you to give me your revolver?'

'Take it yourself. It's in the top drawer of my dressing table.'

He went into the bedroom, where everything was pale pink. The two rooms, one blue, one pink, were reminiscent of a painting by Marie Laurencin.

The bed, a big, low Louis XVI-style bed, was still unmade. The furniture was painted pale grey. On the dressing table were pots of cream, bottles, the whole array of products that women use to fight the ravages of time.

He shrugged. This intimate display saddened him. He thought of Gus writing the first letter.

Without his intervention, would things have happened in the same way?

He took the revolver from the drawer, where there were also jewel boxes.

He didn't know what answer to give the question. Would Madame Parendon have attacked her husband instead of his secretary? Or would she have waited a few more days? Would she have used a different weapon?

He frowned as he went back into the boudoir, where Madame Parendon was standing by the window with her back to him. He realized that this back was starting to stoop. The shoulders struck him as narrower and bonier.

He had the gun in his hand.

'I'll be quite honest with you,' he said. 'I can't establish anything yet, but I'm convinced that when you walked across the drawing room just after nine thirty, this revolver was in the pocket of your dressing gown. I even wonder if it wasn't your husband you were intending to kill at that point. The testimony of the invalid in Rue du Cirque may make it possible to prove that. I assume you approached the door. You heard voices, because your husband was conferring with René Tortu. That's when it occurred to you to perform a kind of substitution. Wouldn't it affect your husband just as profoundly, if not more profoundly, if you killed Antoinette Vague rather than him? Not to mention the fact that, in doing so, you also made him a suspect.

'After we first spoke yesterday, you prepared the ground. You continued today. On the pretext of looking for a stamp, or writing paper, or whatever, you went into her office. She greeted you distractedly and then bent over her work again. You spotted the scalpel and realized there was no point in using the revolver. It would have been too noisy anyway, and someone might have heard.'

He fell silent, lit his pipe as if reluctantly and stood there, waiting, having slipped the mother-of-pearl gun into his pocket. Time passed. Madame Parendon's shoulders had stopped moving. She wasn't crying. She still had her back to him. When she finally turned to look at him, her face was pale and frozen.

Nobody, looking at her, could have suspected what had happened that day on Avenue Marigny, let alone what had just happened in the blue boudoir.

'I'm not mad,' she said emphatically.

He didn't reply. What was the point? What did he know anyway?

8.

'Get dressed, madame,' he said softly. 'You can also pack a suitcase with spare underwear and personal objects. Perhaps you'd better call Lise.'

'To be sure I won't commit suicide? There's no danger of that, don't worry, but go ahead, press the button on your right.'

He waited for Lise to arrive.

'You're going to help Madame Parendon.'

Then he walked slowly along the corridor, head bowed towards the carpet. Losing his way after mistaking one corridor for another, he spotted Ferdinand and Madame Vauquin in the kitchen with the glass door. In front of Ferdinand, there was about half a litre bottle of red wine, from which he had just poured himself a glass. He sat with his elbows on the table, reading a newspaper.

Maigret went in.

They both jumped, and Ferdinand sprang to his feet.

'Can I have a glass?'

'I brought the other bottle back from the office.'

What did it matter? At this point, an old Saint-Émilion or a cheap red . . .

He didn't dare say that he would have preferred the cheap red.

He drank slowly, staring into space. He didn't protest when Ferdinand refilled his glass.

'Where are my men?'

'By the cloakroom. They didn't want to sit in the drawing room.'

Instinctively, they were guarding the exit.

'Lucas, go back to the corridor where you came to see me earlier. Stay outside the door of the boudoir and wait for me.'

He went back to Ferdinand.

'Is the chauffeur in the house?'

'Do you need him? I'll call him right away.'

'What I want is for him to have the car ready under the archway in a few minutes. Are there any reporters in the street?'

'Yes, monsieur.'

'Photographers, too?'

'Yes.'

He knocked at the door of Parendon's office. Parendon was alone, looking through scattered papers and annotating them in red pencil. Seeing Maigret, he sat there motionless and looked at him without daring to ask him any questions. Behind the thick lenses, his blue eyes had an expression that was both gentle and of a sadness that Maigret had seldom encountered.

Did he need to speak? Parendon had understood. While waiting for Maigret, he had clung to his papers as if to a piece of flotsam.

'I think you're going to have the opportunity to study Article 64 a little more, Monsieur Parendon.'

'Has she confessed?'

'Not yet.'

'Do you think she will?'

'The time will come, tonight, in ten days, in a month, when she'll crack, and I prefer not to be there when it happens.'

Parendon took his handkerchief from his pocket and started cleaning the lenses of his glasses as if it were an operation of major importance. As he did so, his pupils seemed to melt into the whites of his eyes. Only his mouth was left to express an almost childlike emotion.

'Are you taking her away?'

The voice was barely audible.

'To avoid comments from the reporters and for her departure to be at least slightly dignified, she'll take her car. I'll give instructions to the chauffeur, and we'll get to Quai des Orfèvres at the same time.'

Parendon looked at him gratefully.

'Don't you want to see her?' Maigret asked, although he suspected the answer.

'To say what?'

'I know. You're right. Are the children here?'

'Gus is at school. I don't know if Bambi's in her room or if she has a class this afternoon.'

Maigret thought both of the one who was about to leave and those who were staying. Life was going to be difficult for them, too, at least for a while.

'Did she say anything about me?'

He asked the question shyly, almost timidly.

'She said a lot about you.'

172

Maigret realized now that it wasn't in books that Madame Parendon had found the words that seemed to accuse her husband. It was in herself. She had performed a kind of transfer, projecting her own disturbance on to him.

He glanced at the clock.

'I'm giving her time to get dressed and pack a suitcase,' he explained. 'Lise is with her.'

. . . if the accused was in a state of insanity at the time of the act, or if he was compelled by a force he was unable to . . .

Men he had arrested because it was his job had been acquitted in court, others sentenced. Some, especially early in his career, had been condemned to death, and two of them had asked him to be there at the last moment.

He had started by studying medicine. He had always regretted having to give up his studies because of circumstances. If he had been able to continue, wouldn't he have chosen psychiatry?

Then he would have been the one to answer the question:

. . . if the accused was in a state of insanity at the time of the act, or if he was compelled by a force he was unable to . . .

Perhaps he didn't regret the interruption of his studies so much. He wouldn't have to decide.

Parendon stood up, came towards him hesitantly, awk-wardly, and held out his little hand.

'I . . .'

But he couldn't speak. They merely shook hands in silence, looking each other in the eyes. Then Maigret walked to the door and closed it behind him without turn-ing round.

He was surprised to see Lucas with Torrence by the exit. A glance from Lucas in the direction of the drawing room made it clear why he had left his post in the corridor.

Madame Parendon was standing there in the middle of the vast room, dressed in a light-coloured tailored suit, a white hat and white gloves. Behind her stood Lise, holding a suitcase.

'Go to the car, both of you, and wait for me.'

He felt like a master of ceremonies, and he knew that he was always going to hate the moment he was living through now.

He advanced towards Madame Parendon and bowed slightly. It was she who spoke, in a calm, natural voice.

'I'll follow you.'

Lise went down with them in the lift. The chauffeur rushed to open the door and was surprised when Maigret didn't get in the car behind his mistress.

He went and put the suitcase in the boot.

'I want you to take Madame Parendon straight to 36 Quai des Orfèvres, drive through the archway and turn left in the courtyard.'

'Very well, inspector.'

Maigret gave the car time to get through the line of reporters and photographers, who couldn't figure out what was going on. Then, as they bombarded him with questions, he joined Lucas and Torrence in the little black police car.

'Will you be making an arrest, Monsieur Maigret?'

'I don't know.'

'Have you identified the guilty party?'

'I don't know, boys.'

He was being honest. The words of Article 64 came back into his mind, one by one, terrifying in their lack of precision.

The sun was still shining, the chestnut trees were still turning green, and he recognized the same figures prowling around the president's palace.

OTHER TITLES IN THE SERIES

MAIGRET AND THE GOOD PEOPLE OF MONTPARNASSE
GEORGES SIMENON

'Why all of a sudden did this shock him? He was annoyed with himself for being shocked. He felt as if he had been sucked into the bourgeois, almost edifying, atmosphere that surrounded those people, "good people" so everyone kept telling him.'

When a seemingly decent man is found shot dead in his family home, Maigret must look beyond the calm, well-to-do exterior of his exemplary life to find the truth.

Translated by Ros Schwartz

INSPECTOR MAIGRET

OTHER TITLES IN THE SERIES

MAIGRET AND THE SATURDAY CALLER
GEORGES SIMENON

'I followed you. Last Saturday, I nearly came up to you in the street, then I thought that wasn't the right place. Not for the kind of conversation I wanted to have. Not in your office either. Perhaps you'll understand . . .'

When Maigret is followed home by a man who confesses he intends to commit a crime, he tries to dissuade this strange visitor, but a subsequent disappearance casts an ominous new light on events.

Translated by Sian Reynolds

OTHER TITLES IN THE SERIES

MAIGRET'S ANGER
GEORGES SIMENON

'There was a dressing table painted grey and cluttered with jars of cream, make-up, eyeliner. The room had a stale, faintly sickly smell. This was where the performers swapped their everyday clothes for their professional gear before stepping out into the spotlights, out to where men bought champagne at five or six times the going rate for the privilege of admiring them.'

Maigret is perplexed by the murder of a Montmartre nightclub owner, until he uncovers a crime much closer to home that threatens his own reputation.

Translated by Will Hobson

OTHER TITLES IN THE SERIES

MAIGRET AND THE GHOST
GEORGES SIMENON

'It wasn't a traditional painter's smock that Madame Jonker was wearing.
It was more a monk's habit, the fabric as thick and soft as a bathrobe.

The Dutchman's wife also wore a white turban of the same fabric
around her head.

She was holding a palette in her left hand, a brush in her right, and
her black eyes lighted on Maigret with curiosity.'

The shooting of a fellow inspector and the disappearance of a key
witness lead Maigret to some disturbing discoveries about an
esteemed Paris art critic.

Translated by Ros Schwartz

INSPECTOR MAIGRET

OTHER TITLES IN THE SERIES

MAIGRET DEFENDS HIMSELF
GEORGES SIMENON

'Maigret's cheeks turned red, as they had at school whenever he was called to the headmaster's office. 28 June ... He had been in the Police Judiciaire for more than thirty years, and the head of the Crime Squad for ten years, but this was the first time he had been summoned like this.'

When Maigret is shocked to find himself accused of a crime, he must fight to prove his innocence and save his reputation.

Translated by Howard Curtis

INSPECTOR MAIGRET

OTHER TITLES IN THE SERIES

MAIGRET'S PATIENCE
GEORGES SIMENON

'Maigret felt less light at heart than when he had woken up that morning with sunlight streaming into his apartment or when he had stood on the bus platform, soaking up images of Paris coloured like in a children's album. People were often very keen to ask him about his methods. Some even thought they could analyse them, and he would look at them with mocking curiosity.'

When a gangster Maigret has been investigating for years is found dead in his apartment, the Inspector continues to bide his time and explore every angle until he finally reaches the truth.

Translated by David Watson

OTHER TITLES IN THE SERIES

MAIGRET AND THE NAHOUR CASE
GEORGES SIMENON

'*Maigret had often been called on to deal with individuals of this sort, who were equally at home in London, New York and Rome, who took planes the way other people took the Metro, who stayed in grand hotels . . . he had trouble suppressing feelings of irritation that might have been taken for jealousy.*'

A professional gambler has been shot dead in his elegant Parisian home, and his enigmatic wife seems the most likely culprit – but Inspector Maigret suspects this notorious case is far more complicated than it appears.

Translated by Will Hobson

OTHER TITLES IN THE SERIES

MAIGRET'S PICKPOCKET
GEORGES SIMENON

'Maigret would have found it difficult to formulate an opinion of him. Intelligent, yes, certainly, and highly so, as far as one could tell from what lay beneath some of his utterances. Yet alongside that, there was a naïve, rather childish side to him.'

Maigret is savouring a beautiful spring morning in Paris when an aspiring film-maker draws his attention to a much less inspiring scene, one where ever changing loyalties can have tragic consequences.

Translated by Sian Reynolds

OTHER TITLES IN THE SERIES